W.W. JACOBS – THE SHORT STORIES
VOLUME 1

William Wymark Jacobs was born on September 8th, 1863 in the Wapping district of London, England. Jacobs grew up near the docks, where his father was a wharf manager. The docks and river side would be a constant theme of his writing in years to come.

Although surrounded by poverty, he received a formal education in London, first at a private prep school and later at the Birkbeck Literary and Scientific Institute.

His working life began with a less than exciting clerical position at the Post Office Savings Bank. Jacobs put his imagination to good use writing short stories, sketches and articles, many for the Post Office house publication "Blackfriars Magazine."

In 1896 Jacobs published Many Cargoes, a selection of sea-faring yarns, which established him as a popular writer with a knack for authentic dialogue and trick endings.

A year later he published a novelette, The Skipper's Wooing, and in 1898 another collection of short stories; Sea Urchins. These works painted vivid pictures of dockland and seafaring London full of colourful characters.

By 1899, Jacobs was able to quit the post office and write full-time.

He married the noted suffragist Agnes Eleanor Williams (who had been jailed for her protest activities) in 1900. They set up households both in Loughton, Essex and in central London.

The publication in 1902 of At Sunwich Port and Dialstone Lane, in 1904, cemented Jacobs' reputation as one of the leading British authors of the new century.

There followed a string of further successful publications, including Captain's All (1905), Night Watches (1914), The Castaways (1916), and Sea Whispers (1926).

Though Jacobs would create little in the way of new work after 1911, he still wrote and was recognized as a leading humorist, ranked alongside such writers as P. G. Wodehouse.

William Wymark Jacobs died in a North London nursing home in Hornsey Lane, Islington on September 1st, 1943.

Index of Contents
A BENEFIT PERFORMANCE
A BLACK AFFAIR
A CASE OF DESERTION
A CHANGE OF TREATMENT
A CIRCULAR TOUR
A DISCIPLINARIAN
A DISTANT RELATIVE
A GARDEN PLOT

A GOLDEN VENTURE
A HARBOUR OF REFUGE
A LOVE KNOT
A LOVE PASSAGE
A MARKED MAN
A MIXED PROPOSAL
W.W. JACOBS – A SHORT BIOGRAPHY
W.W. JACOBS – A CONCISE BIBLIOGRAPHY

A BENEFIT PERFORMANCE

In the small front parlour of No. 3, Mermaid Passage, Sunset Bay, Jackson Pepper, ex-pilot, sat in a state of indignant collapse, tenderly feeling a cheek on which the print of hasty fingers still lingered.

The room, which was in excellent order, showed no signs of the tornado which had passed through it, and Jackson Pepper, looking vaguely round, was dimly reminded of those tropical hurricanes he had read about which would strike only the objects in the path, and leave all others undisturbed.

In this instance he had been the object, and the tornado, after obliterating him, had passed up the small staircase which led from the room, leaving him listening anxiously to its distant mutterings.

To his great discomfort the storm showed signs of coming up again, and he had barely time to effect an appearance of easy unconcern, which accorded but ill with the flush afore-mentioned, when a big, red-faced woman came heavily downstairs and burst into the room.

"You have made me ill again," she said severely, "and now I hope you are satisfied with your work. You'll kill me before you have done with me!"

The ex-pilot shifted on his chair.

"You're not fit to have a wife," continued Mrs. Pepper, "aggravating them and upsetting them! Any other woman would have left you long ago!"

"We've only been married three months," Pepper reminded her.

"Don't talk to me!" said his wife; "it seems more like a lifetime!"

"It seems a long time to ME" said the ex-pilot, plucking up a little courage.

"That's right!" said his wife, striding over to where he sat. "Say you're tired of me; say you wish you hadn't married me! You coward! Ah! if my poor first husband was only alive and sitting in that chair now instead of you, how happy I would be!"

"If he likes to come and take it he's welcome!" said Pepper; "it's my chair, and it was my father's before me, but there's no man living I would sooner give it to than your first. Ah! he knew what he was about when the Dolphin went down, he did. I don't blame him, though."

"What do you mean?" demanded his wife.

"It's my belief that he didn't go down with her," said Pepper, crossing over to the staircase and standing with his hand on the door.

"Didn't go down with her?" repeated his wife scornfully. "What became of him, then? Where's he been this thirty years?"

"In hiding!" said Pepper spitefully, and passed hastily upstairs.

The room above was charged with memories of the late lamented. His portrait in oils hung above the mantel-piece, smaller portraits—specimens of the photographer's want of art—were scattered about the room, while various personal effects, including a mammoth pair of sea-boots, stood in a corner. On all these articles the eye of Jackson Pepper dwelt with an air of chastened regret.

"It 'ud be a rum go if he did turn up after all," he said to himself softly, as he sat on the edge of the bed. "I've heard of such things in books. I dessay she'd be disappointed if she did see him now. Thirty years makes a bit of difference in a man."

"Jackson!" cried his wife from below, "I'm going out. If you want any dinner you can get it; if not, you can go without it!"

The front door slammed violently, and Jackson, advancing cautiously to the window, saw the form of his wife sailing majestically up the passage. Then he sat down again and resumed his meditations.

"If it wasn't for leaving all my property I'd go," he said gloomily. "There's not a bit of comfort in the place! Nag, nag, nag, from morn till night! Ah, Cap'n Budd, you let me in for a nice thing when you went down with that boat of yours. Come back and fill them boots again; they're too big for me."

He rose suddenly and stood gaping in the centre of the room, as a mad, hazy idea began to form in his brain. His eyes blinked and his face grew white with excitement. He pushed open the little lattice window, and sat looking abstractedly up the passage on to the bay beyond. Then he put on his hat, and, deep in thought, went out.

He was still thinking deeply as he boarded the train for London next morning, and watched Sunset Bay from the window until it disappeared round the curve. So many and various were the changes that flitted over his face that an old lady, whose seat he had taken, gave up her intention of apprising him of the fact, and indulged instead in a bitter conversation with her daughter, of which the erring Pepper was the unconscious object.

In the same preoccupied fashion he got on a Bayswater omnibus, and waited patiently for it to reach Poplar. Strange changes in the landscape, not to be accounted for by the mere lapse of time, led to explanations, and the conductor—a humane man, who said he had got an idiot boy at home—personally laid down the lines of his tour. Two hours later he stood in front of a small house painted in many colours, and, ringing the bell, inquired for Cap'n Crippen.

In response to his inquiry, a big man, with light blue eyes and a long grey beard, appeared, and, recognising his visitor with a grunt of surprise, drew him heartily into the passage and thrust him into the parlour. He then shook hands with him, and, clapping him on the back, bawled lustily for the small boy who had opened the door.

"Pot o' stout, bottle o' gin, and two long pipes," said he, as the boy came to the door and eyed the ex-pilot curiously.

At all these honest preparations for his welcome the heart of Jackson grew faint within him.

"Well, I call it good of you to come all this way to see me," said the captain, after the boy had disappeared; "but you always was warm-hearted, Pepper. And how's the missis?"

"Shocking!" said Pepper, with a groan.

"Ill?" inquired the captain.

"Ill-tempered," said Pepper. "In fact, cap'n, I don't mind telling you, she's killing me—slowly killing me!"

"Pooh!" said Crippen. "Nonsense! You don't know how to manage her!"

"I thought perhaps you could advise me," said the artful Pepper. "I said to myself yesterday, 'Pepper, go and see Cap'n Crippen. What he don't know about wimmen and their management ain't worth knowing! If there's anybody can get you out of a hole, it's him. He's got the power, and, what's more, he's got the will!'"

"What causes the temper?" inquired the captain, with his most judicial air, as he took the liquor from his messenger and carefully filled a couple of glasses.

"It's natural!" said his friend ruefully. "She calls it having a high spirit herself. And she's so generous. She's got a married niece living in the place, and when that gal comes round and admires the things—my things—she gives 'em to her! She gave her a sofa the other day, and, what's more, she made me help the gal to carry it home!"

"Have you tried being sarcastic?" inquired the captain thoughtfully.

"I have," said Pepper, with a shiver. "The other day I said, very nasty, 'Is there anything else you'd like, my dear?' but she didn't understand it."

"No?" said the captain.

"No," said Pepper. "She said I was very kind, and she'd like the clock; and, what's more, she had it too! Red-'aired hussy!"

The captain poured out some gin and drank it slowly. It was evident he was thinking deeply, and that he was much affected by his friend's troubles.

"There is only one way for me to get clear," said Pepper, as he finished a thrilling recital of his wrongs, "and that is, to find Cap'n Budd, her first."

"Why, he's dead!" said Crippen, staring hard. "Don't you waste your time looking for him!"

"I'm not going to," said Pepper; "but here's his portrait. He was a big man like you; he had blue eyes and a straight handsome nose, like you. If he'd lived to now he'd be almost your age, and very likely more like you than ever. He was a sailor; you've been a sailor."

The captain stared at him in bewilderment.

"He had a wonderful way with wimmen," pursued Jackson hastily; "you've got a wonderful way with wimmen. More than that, you've got the most wonderful gift for acting I've ever seen. Ever since the time when you acted in that barn at Bristol I've never seen any actor I can honestly say I've liked—never! Look how you can imitate cats—better than Henry Irving himself!"

"I never had much chance, being at sea all my life," said Crippen modestly.

"You've got the gift," said Pepper impressively. "It was born in you, and you'll never leave off acting till the day of your death. You couldn't if you tried—you know you couldn't!"

The captain smiled deprecatingly.

"Now, I want you to do a performance for my benefit," continued Pepper. "I want you to act Cap'n Budd, what was lost in the Dolphin thirty years ago. There's only one man in England I'd trust with the part, and that's you."

"Act Cap'n Budd!" gasped the astonished Crippen, putting down his glass and staring at his friend.

"The part is written here," said the ex-pilot, producing a note-book from his breast pocket and holding it out to his friend. I've been keeping a log day by day of all the things she said about him, in the hopes of catching her tripping, but I never did. There's notes of his family, his ships, and a lot of silly things he used to say, which she thinks funny."

"I couldn't do it!" said the captain seriously, as he took the book.

"You could do it if you liked," said Pepper. "Besides, think what a spree it'll be for you. Learn it by heart, then come down and claim her. Her name's Martha."

"What good 'ud it do you if I did?" inquired the captain. "She'd soon find out!"

"You come down to Sunset Bay," said Pepper, emphasising his remarks with his forefinger; "you claim your wife; you allude carefully to the things set down in this book; I give Martha back to you and bless you both. Then—"

"Then what?" inquired Crippen anxiously.

"You disappear!" concluded Pepper triumphantly; "and, of course, believing her first husband is alive, she has to leave me. She's a very particular woman; and, besides that, I'd take care to let the neighbours know. I'm happy, you're happy, and, if she's not happy, why, she don't deserve to be."

"I'll think it over," said Crippen, "and write and let you know."

"Make up your mind now," urged Pepper, reaching over and patting him encouragingly upon the shoulder. "If you promise to do it, the thing's as good as done. Lord! I think I see you now, coming in at that door and surprising her. Talk about acting!"

"Is she what you'd call a good-looking woman?" inquired Crippen.

"Very handsome!" said Pepper, looking out of the window.

"I couldn't do it!" said the captain. "It wouldn't be right and fair to her."

"I don't see that!" said Pepper. "I never ought to have married her without being certain her first was dead. It ain't right, Crippen; say what you like, it ain't right!"

"If you put it that way," said the captain hesitatingly.

"Have some more gin," said the artful pilot.

The captain had some more, and, what with flattery and gin, combined with the pleadings of his friend, began to consider the affair more favourably. Pepper stuck to his guns, and used them so well that when the captain saw him off that evening he was pledged up to the hilt to come down to Sunset Bay and personate the late Captain Budd on the following Thursday.

The ex-pilot passed the intervening days in a sort of trance, from which he only emerged to take nourishment, or answer the scoldings of his wife. On the eventful Thursday, however, his mood changed, and he went about in such a state of suppressed excitement that he could scarcely keep still.

"Lor' bless me!" snapped Mrs. Pepper, as he slowly perambulated the parlour that afternoon. "What ails the man? Can't you keep still for five minutes?"

The ex-pilot stopped and eyed her solemnly, but, ere he could reply, his heart gave a great bound, for, from behind the geraniums which filled the window, he saw the face of Captain Crippen slowly rise and peer cautiously into the room. Before his wife could follow the direction of her husband's eyes it had disappeared.

"Somebody looking in at the window," said Pepper, with forced calmness, in reply to his wife's eyebrows.

"Like their impudence!" said the unconscious woman, resuming her knitting, while her husband waited in vain for the captain to enter.

He waited some time, and then, half dead with excitement, sat down, and with shaking fingers lit his pipe. As he looked up the stalwart figure of the captain passed the window. During the next twenty minutes it passed seven times, and Pepper, coming to the not unnatural conclusion that his friend intended to pass the afternoon in the same unprofitable fashion, resolved to force his hand.

"Must be a tramp," he said aloud.

"Who?" inquired his wife. "Man keeps looking in at the window," said Pepper desperately. "Keeps looking in till he meets my eye, then he disappears. Looks like an old sea-captain, something."

"Old sea-captain?" said his wife, putting down her work and turning round. There was a strange hesitating note in her voice. She looked at the window, and at the same instant the head of the captain again appeared above the geraniums, and, meeting her gaze, hastily vanished. Martha Pepper sat still for a moment, and then, rising in a slow, dazed fashion, crossed to the door and opened it. Mermaid Passage was empty!

"See anybody?" quavered Pepper.

His wife shook her head, but in a strangely quiet fashion, and, sitting down, took up her knitting again.

For some time the click of the needles and the tick of the clock were the only sounds audible, and the ex-pilot had just arrived at the conclusion that his friend had abandoned him to his fate, when there came a low tapping at the door.

"Come in!" cried Pepper, starting.

The door opened slowly, and the tall figure of Captain Crippen entered and stood there eyeing them nervously. A neat little speech he had prepared failed him at the supreme moment. He leaned against the wall, and in a clumsy, shamefaced fashion lowered his gaze, and stammered out the one word—"Martha!"

At that word Mrs. Pepper rose and stood with parted lips, eyeing him wildly.

"Jem!" she gasped, "Jem!"

"Martha!" croaked the captain again.

With a choking cry Mrs. Pepper ran towards him, and, to the huge gratification of her lawful spouse, flung her arms about his neck and kissed him violently.

"Jem," she cried breathlessly, "is it really you? I can hardly believe it. Where have you been all this long time? Where have you been?"

"Lots of places," said the captain, who was not prepared to answer a question like that offhand; "but wherever I've been"—he held up his hand theatrically—"the image of my dear lost wife has been always in front of me."

"I knew you at once, Jem," said Mrs. Pepper fondly, smoothing the hair back from his forehead. "Have I altered much?"

"Not a bit," said Crippen, holding her at arm's length and carefully regarding her. "You look just the same as the first time I set eyes on you."

"Where have you been?" wailed Martha Pepper, putting her head on his shoulder.

"When the Dolphin went down from under me, and left me fighting with the waves for life and Martha, I was cast ashore on a desert island," began Crippen fluently. "There I remained for nearly three years, when I was rescued by a barque bound for New South Wales. There I met a man from Poole who told me you were dead. Having no further interest in the land of my birth, I sailed in Australian waters for many years, and it was only lately that I heard how cruelly I had been deceived, and that my little flower was still blooming."

The little flower's head being well down on his shoulder again, the celebrated actor exchanged glances with the worshipping Pepper.

"If you'd only come before, Jem," said Mrs. Pepper. "Who was he? What was his name?"

"Smith," said the cautious captain.

"If you'd only come before, Jem," said Mrs. Pepper, in a smothered voice, "it would have been better. Only three months ago I married that object over there."

The captain attempted a melodramatic start with such success, that, having somewhat underestimated the weight of his fair bride, he nearly lost his balance.

"It can't be helped, I suppose," he said reproachfully, "but you might have waited a little longer, Martha."

"Well, I'm your wife, anyhow," said Martha, "and I'll take care I never lose you again. You shall never go out of my sight again till you die. Never."

"Nonsense, my pet," said the captain, exchanging uneasy glances with the ex-pilot. "Nonsense."

"It isn't nonsense, Jem," said the lady, as she drew him on to the sofa and sat with her arms round his neck. "It may be true, all you've told me, and it may not. For all I know, you may have been married to some other woman; but I've got you now, and I intend to keep you."

"There, there," said the captain, as soothingly as a strange sinking at the heart would allow him.

"As for that other little man, I only married him because he worried me so," said Mrs. Pepper tearfully. "I never loved him, but he used to follow me about and propose. Was it twelve or thirteen times you proposed to me, Pepper?"

"I forget," said the ex-pilot shortly.

"But I never loved him," she continued. "I never loved you a bit, did I, Pepper?"

"Not a bit," said Pepper warmly. "No man could ever have a harder or more unfeeling wife than you was. I'll say that for you, willing."

As he bore this testimony to his wife's fidelity there was a knock at the door, and, upon his opening it, the rector's daughter, a lady of uncertain age, entered, and stood regarding with amazement the frantic but ineffectual struggles of Captain Crippen to release himself from a position as uncomfortable as it was ridiculous.

"Mrs. Pepper!" said the lady, aghast. "Oh, Mrs. Pepper!"

"It's all right, Miss Winthrop," said the lady addressed, calmly, as she forced the captain's flushed face on to her ample shoulder again; "it's my first husband, Jem Budd."

"Good gracious!" said Miss Winthrop, starting. "Enoch Arden in the flesh!"

"Who?" inquired Pepper, with a show of polite interest.

"Enoch Arden," said Miss Winthrop. "One of our great poets wrote a noble poem about a sailor who came home and found that his wife had married again; but, in the POEM, the first husband went away without making himself known, and died of a broken heart."

She looked at Captain Crippen as though he hadn't quite come up to her expectations.

"And now," said Pepper, speaking with great cheerfulness, "it's me that's got to have the broken heart. Well, well."

"It's a most interesting case," cried Miss Winthrop; "and, if you wait till I fetch my camera, I'll take your portrait together just as you are."

"Do," said Mrs. Pepper cordially.

"I won't have my portrait took," said the captain, with much acerbity.

"Not if I wish it, dear?" inquired Mrs. Pepper tenderly.

"Not if you keep a-wishing it all your life," replied the captain sourly, making another attempt to get his head from her shoulder.

"Don't you think they ought to have their portrait taken now?" asked Miss Winthrop, turning to the ex-pilot.

"I don't see no 'arm in it," said Pepper thoughtlessly.

"You hear what Mr. Pepper says," said the lady, turning to the captain again. "Surely if he doesn't mind, you ought not to."

"I'll talk to him by-and-bye," said the captain, very grimly.

"P'raps it would be better if we kept this affair to ourselves for the present," said the ex-pilot, taking alarm at his friend's manner.

"Well, I won't intrude on you any longer," said Miss Winthrop. "Oh! Look there! How rude of them!"

The others turned hastily in time to see several heads vanish from the window. Captain Crippen was the first to speak.

"Jem!" said Mrs. Pepper severely, before he had finished.

"Captain Budd!" said Miss Winthrop, flushing.

The incensed captain rose to his feet and paced up and down the room. He looked at the ex-pilot, and that small schemer shivered.

"Easy does it, cap'n," he murmured, with a wink which he meant to be comforting.

"I'm going out a little way," said the captain, after the rector's daughter had gone. "Just to cool my head."

Mrs. Pepper took her bonnet from its peg behind the door, and, surveying herself in the glass, tied it beneath her chin.

"Alone," said Crippen nervously. "I want to do a little thinking."

"Never again, Jem," said Mrs. Pepper firmly. "My place is by your side. If you're ashamed of people looking at you, I'm not. I'm proud of you. Come along. Come and show yourself, and tell them who you are. You shall never go out of my sight again as long as I live. Never."

She began to whimper.

"What's to be done?" inquired Crippen, turning desperately on the bewildered pilot.

"What's it got to do with him?" demanded Mrs. Pepper sharply.

"He's got to be considered a little, I s'pose," said the captain, dissembling. "Besides, I think I'd better do like the man in the poetry did. Let me go away and die of a broken heart. Perhaps it's best."

Mrs. Pepper looked at him with kindling eyes.

"Let me go away and die of a broken heart," repeated the captain, with real feeling. "I'd rather do it. I would indeed."

Mrs. Pepper, bursting into angry tears, flung her arms round his neck again, and sobbed on his shoulder. The pilot, obeying the frenzied injunctions of his friend's eye, drew down the blind.

"There's quite a crowd outside," he remarked.

"I don't mind," said his wife amiably. "They'll soon know who he is."

She stood holding the captain's hand and stroking it, and whenever his feelings became too much for her put her head down on his waistcoat. At such times the captain glared fiercely at the ex-pilot, who, being of a weak nature, was unable, despite his anxiety, to give his risible faculties that control which the solemnity of the occasion demanded.

The afternoon wore slowly away. Miss Winthrop, who disliked scandal, had allowed something of the affair to leak out, and several visitors, including a local reporter, called, but were put off till the morrow, on the not unnatural plea that the long-separated couple desired a little privacy. The three sat silent, the ex-pilot, with wrinkled brows, trying hard to decipher the lip-language in which the captain addressed him whenever he had an opportunity, but could only dimly guess its purport, when the captain pressed his huge fist into the service as well.

Mrs. Pepper rose at length, and went into the back room to prepare tea. As she left the door open, however, and took the captain's hat with her, he built no hopes on her absence, but turned furiously to the ex-pilot.

"What's to be done?" he inquired in a fierce whisper. "This can't go on."

"It'll have to," whispered the other.

"Now, look here," said Crippen menacingly, "I'm going into the kitchen to make a clean breast of it. I'm sorry for you, but I've done the best I can. Come and help me to explain."

He turned to the kitchen, but the other, with the strength born of despair, seized him by the sleeve and held him back.

"She'll kill me," he whispered breathlessly.

"I can't help it," said Crippen, shaking him off. "Serve you right."

"And she'll tell the folks outside, and they'll kill you," continued Pepper.

The captain sat down again, and confronted him with a face as pale as his own.

"The last train leaves at eight," whispered the pilot hurriedly. "It's desperate, but it's the only thing you can do. Take her for a stroll up by the fields near the railway station. You can see the train coming in for a mile off nearly. Time yourself carefully, and make a bolt for it. She can't run."

The entrance of their victim with the tea-tray stopped the conversation; but the captain nodded acceptance behind her back, and then, with a forced gaiety, sat down to tea.

For the first time since his successful appearance he became loquacious, and spoke so freely of incidents in the life of the man he was impersonating that the ex-pilot sat in a perfect fever lest he should blunder. The meal finished, he proposed a stroll, and, as the unsuspecting Mrs. Pepper tied on her bonnet, slapped his leg, and winked confidently at his fellow-conspirator.

"I'm not much of a walker," said the innocent Mrs. Pepper, "so you must go slowly."

The captain nodded, and at Pepper's suggestion left by the back way, to avoid the gaze of the curious.

For some time after their departure Pepper sat smoking, with his anxious face turned to the clock, until at length, unable to endure the strain any longer, and not without a sportsmanlike idea of being in at the death, he made his way to the station, and placed himself behind a convenient coal-truck.

He waited impatiently, with his eyes fixed on the road up which he expected the captain to come. He looked at his watch. Five minutes to eight, and still no captain. The platform began to fill, a porter seized the big bell and rang it lustily; in the distance a patch of white smoke showed. Just as the watcher had given up all hope, the figure of the captain came in sight. He was swaying from side to side, holding his hat in his hand, but doggedly racing the train to the station.

"He'll never do it!" groaned the pilot. Then he held his breath, for three or four hundred yards behind the captain Mrs. Pepper pounded in pursuit.

The train rolled into the station; passengers stepped in and out; doors slammed, and the guard had already placed the whistle in his mouth, when Captain Crippen, breathing stentorously, came stumbling blindly on to the platform, and was hustled into a third class carriage.

"Close shave that, sir," said the station-master as he closed the door.

The captain sank back in his seat, fighting for breath, and turning his head, gave a last triumphant look up the road.

"All right, sir," said the station-master kindly, as he followed the direction of the other's eyes and caught sight of Mrs. Pepper. "We'll wait for your lady."

Jackson Pepper came from behind the coal-truck and watched the train out of sight, wondering in a dull, vague fashion what the conversation was like. He stood so long that a tender hearted porter, who had heard the news, made bold to come up and put a friendly hand on his shoulder.

"You'll never see her again, Mr. Pepper," he said sympathetically.

The ex-pilot turned and regarded him fixedly, and the last bit of spirit he was ever known to show flashed up in his face as he spoke.

"You're a blamed idiot!" he said rudely.

A BLACK AFFAIR

"I didn't want to bring it," said Captain Gubson, regarding somewhat unfavourably a grey parrot whose cage was hanging against the mainmast, "but my old uncle was so set on it I had to. He said a sea-voyage would set its 'elth up."

"It seems to be all right at present," said the mate, who was tenderly sucking his forefinger; "best of spirits, I should say."

"It's playful," assented the skipper. "The old man thinks a rare lot of it. I think I shall have a little bit in that quarter, so keep your eye on the beggar."

"Scratch Poll!" said the parrot, giving its bill a preliminary strop on its perch. "Scratch poor Polly!"

It bent its head against the bars, and waited patiently to play off what it had always regarded as the most consummate practical joke in existence. The first doubt it had ever had about it occurred when the mate came forward and obligingly scratched it with the stem of his pipe.

It was a wholly unforeseen development, and the parrot, ruffling its feathers, edged along its perch and brooded darkly at the other end of it.

Opinion before the mast was also against the new arrival, the general view being that the wild jealousy which raged in the bosom of the ship's cat would sooner or later lead to mischief.

"Old Satan don't like it," said the cook, shaking his head. "The blessed bird hadn't been aboard ten minutes before Satan was prowling around.

The blooming image waited till he was about a foot off the cage, and then he did the perlite and asked him whether he'd like a glass o' beer.

"I never see a cat so took aback in all my life. Never."

"There'll be trouble between 'em," said old Sam, who was the cat's special protector, "mark my words."

"I'd put my money on the parrot," said one of the men confidently. "It's 'ad a crool bit out of the mate's finger. Where 'ud the cat be agin that beak?"

"Well, you'd lose your money," said Sam. "If you want to do the cat a kindness, every time you see him near that cage cuff his 'ed."

The crew being much attached to the cat, which had been presented to them when a kitten by the mate's wife, acted upon the advice with so much zest that for the next two days the indignant animal was like to have been killed with kindness. On the third day, however, the parrot's cage being on the cabin table, the cat stole furtively down, and, at the pressing request of the occupant itself, scratched its head for it.

The skipper was the first to discover the mischief, and he came on deck and published the news in a voice which struck a chill to all hearts.

"Where's that black devil got to?" he yelled.

"Anything wrong, sir?" asked Sam anxiously.

"Come and look here," said the skipper. He led the way to the cabin, where the mate and one of the crew were already standing, shaking their heads over the parrot.

"What do you make of that?" demanded the skipper fiercely.

"Too much dry food, sir," said Sam, after due deliberation.

"Too much what?" bellowed the skipper.

"Too much dry food," repeated Sam firmly. "A parrot—a grey parrot—wants plenty o' sop. If it don't get it, it moults."

"It's had too much CAT" said the skipper fiercely, "and you know it, and overboard it goes."

"I don't believe it was the cat, sir," interposed the other man; "it's too soft-hearted to do a thing like that."

"You can shut your jaw," said the skipper, reddening. "Who asked you to come down here at all?"

"Nobody saw the cat do it," urged the mate.

The skipper said nothing, but, stooping down, picked up a tail feather from the floor, and laid it on the table. He then went on deck, followed by the others, and began calling, in seductive tones, for the cat. No reply forth coming from the sagacious animal, which had gone into hiding, he turned to Sam, and bade him call it.

"No, sir, I won't 'ave no 'and in it," said the old man. "Putting aside my liking for the animal, I'M not going to 'ave anything to do with the killing of a black cat."

"Rubbish!" said the skipper.

"Very good, sir," said Sam, shrugging his shoulders, "you know best, o' course. You're eddicated and I'm not, an' p'raps you can afford to make a laugh o' such things. I knew one man who killed a black cat an' he went mad. There's something very pecooliar about that cat o' ours."

"It knows more than we do," said one of the crew, shaking his head. "That time you—I mean we—ran the smack down, that cat was expecting of it 'ours before. It was like a wild thing."

"Look at the weather we've 'ad—look at the trips we've made since he's been aboard," said the old man. "Tell me it's chance if you like, but I KNOW better."

The skipper hesitated. He was a superstitious man even for a sailor, and his weakness was so well known that he had become a sympathetic receptacle for every ghost story which, by reason of its crudeness or lack of corroboration, had been rejected by other experts. He was a perfect reference library for omens, and his interpretations of dreams had gained for him a widespread reputation.

"That's all nonsense," he said, pausing uneasily; "still, I only want to be just. There's nothing vindictive about me, and I'll have no hand in it myself. Joe, just tie a lump of coal to that cat and heave it overboard."

"Not me," said the cook, following Sam's lead, and working up a shudder. "Not for fifty pun in gold. I don't want to be haunted."

"The parrot's a little better now, sir," said one of the men, taking advantage of his hesitation, "he's opened one eye."

"Well, I only want to be just," repeated the skipper. "I won't do anything in a hurry, but, mark my words, if the parrot dies that cat goes overboard."

Contrary to expectations, the bird was still alive when London was reached, though the cook, who from his connection with the cabin had suddenly reached a position of unusual importance, reported great loss of strength and irritability of temper. It was still alive, but failing fast on the day they were to put to sea again; and the fo'c'sle, in preparation for the worst, stowed their pet away in the paint-locker, and discussed the situation.

Their council was interrupted by the mysterious behaviour of the cook, who, having gone out to lay in a stock of bread, suddenly broke in upon them more in the manner of a member of a secret society than a humble but useful unit of a ship's company.

"Where's the cap'n?" he asked in a hoarse whisper, as he took a seat on the locker with the sack of bread between his knees.

"In the cabin," said Sam, regarding his antics with some disfavour. "What's wrong, cookie?"

"What d' yer think I've got in here?" asked the cook, patting the bag.

The obvious reply to this question was, of course, bread; but as it was known that the cook had departed specially to buy some, and that he could hardly ask a question involving such a simple answer, nobody gave it.

"It come to me all of a sudden," said the cook, in a thrilling whisper. "I'd just bought the bread and left the shop, when I see a big black cat, the very image of ours, sitting on a doorstep. I just stooped down to stroke its 'ed, when it come to me."

"They will sometimes," said one of the seamen.

"I don't mean that," said the cook, with the contempt of genius. "I mean the idea did. Ses I to myself, 'You might be old Satan's brother by the look of you; an' if the cap'n wants to kill a cat, let it be you,' I ses. And with that, before it could say Jack Robinson, I picked it up by the scruff o' the neck and shoved it in the bag."

"What, all in along of our bread?" said the previous interrupter, in a pained voice.

"Some of yer are 'ard ter please," said the cook, deeply offended.

"Don't mind him, cook," said the admiring Sam. "You're a masterpiece, that's what you are."

"Of course, if any of you've got a better plan"—said the cook generously.

"Don't talk rubbish, cook," said Sam; "fetch the two cats out and put 'em together."

"Don't mix 'em," said the cook warningly; "for you'll never know which is which agin if you do."

He cautiously opened the top of the sack and produced his captive, and Satan, having been relieved from his prison, the two animals were carefully compared.

"They're as like as two lumps o' coal," said Sam slowly. "Lord, what a joke on the old man. I must tell the mate o' this; he'll enjoy it."

"It'll be all right if the parrot don't die," said the dainty pessimist, still harping on his pet theme. "All that bread spoilt, and two cats aboard."

"Don't mind what he ses," said Sam; "you're a brick, that's what you are. I'll just make a few holes in the lid o' the boy's chest, and pop old Satan in. You don't mind, do you, Billy?"

"Of course he don't," said the other men indignantly.

Matters being thus agreeably arranged, Sam got a gimlet, and prepared the chest for the reception of its tenant, who, convinced that he was being put out of the way to make room for a rival, made a frantic fight for freedom.

"Now get something 'eavy and put on the top of it," said Sam, having convinced himself that the lock was broken; "and, Billy, put the noo cat in the paint-locker till we start; it's home-sick."

The boy obeyed, and the understudy was kept in durance vile until they were off Limehouse, when he came on deck and nearly ended his career there and then by attempting to jump over the bulwark into the next garden. For some time he paced the deck in a perturbed fashion, and then, leaping on the stern, mewed plaintively as his native city receded farther and farther from his view.

"What's the matter with old Satan?" said the mate, who had been let into the secret. "He seems to have something on his mind."

"He'll have something round his neck presently," said the skipper grimly.

The prophecy was fulfilled some three hours later, when he came up on deck ruefully regarding the remains of a bird whose vocabulary had once been the pride of its native town. He threw it overboard without a word, and then, seizing the innocent cat, who had followed him under the impression that it was about to lunch, produced half a brick attached to a string, and tied it round his neck. The crew, who were enjoying the joke immensely, raised a howl of protest.

"The Skylark'll never have another like it, sir," said Sam solemnly. "That cat was the luck of the ship."

"I don't want any of your old woman's yarns," said the skipper brutally. "If you want the cat, go and fetch it."

He stepped aft as he spoke, and sent the gentle stranger hurtling through the air. There was a "plomp" as it reached the water, a bubble or two came to the surface, and all was over.

"That's the last o' that," he said, turning away.

The old man shook his head. "You can't kill a black cat for nothing," said he, "mark my words!"

The skipper, who was in a temper at the time, thought little of them, but they recurred to him vividly the next day. The wind had freshened during the night, and rain was falling heavily. On deck the crew stood about in oilskins, while below, the boy, in his new capacity of gaoler, was ministering to the wants of an ungrateful prisoner, when the cook, happening to glance that way, was horrified to see the animal emerge from the fo'c'sle. It eluded easily the frantic clutch of the boy as he sprang up the ladder after it, and walked leisurely along the deck in the direction of the cabin. Just as the crew had given it up for lost it encountered Sam, and the next moment, despite its cries, was caught up and huddled away beneath his stiff clammy oilskins. At the noise the skipper, who was talking to the mate, turned as though he had been shot, and gazed wildly round him.

"Dick," said he, "can you hear a cat?"

"Cat!" said the mate, in accents of great astonishment.

"I thought I heard it," said the puzzled skipper.

"Fancy, sir," said Dick firmly, as a mewing, appalling in its wrath, came from beneath Sam's coat.

"Did you hear it, Sam?" called the skipper, as the old man was moving off.

"Hear what, sir?" inquired Sam respectfully, without turning round.

"Nothing," said the skipper, collecting himself. "Nothing. All right."

The old man, hardly able to believe in his good fortune, made his way forward, and, seizing a favourable opportunity, handed his ungrateful burden back to the boy.

"Fancy you heard a cat just now?" inquired the mate casually.

"Well, between you an' me, Dick," said the skipper, in a mysterious voice, "I did, and it wasn't fancy neither. I heard that cat as plain as if it was alive."

"Well, I've heard of such things," said the other, "but I don't believe 'em. What a lark if the old cat comes back climbing up over the side out of the sea to-night, with the brick hanging round its neck."

The skipper stared at him for some time without speaking. "If that's your idea of a lark," he said at length, in a voice which betrayed traces of some emotion, "it ain't mine."

"Well, if you hear it again," said the mate cordially, "you might let me know. I'm rather interested in such things."

The skipper, hearing no more of it that day, tried hard to persuade himself that he was the victim of imagination, but, in spite of this, he was pleased at night, as he stood at the wheel, to reflect on the sense of companionship afforded by the look-out in the bows. On his part the look-out was quite charmed with the unwonted affability of the skipper, as he yelled out to him two or three times on matters only faintly connected with the progress of the schooner.

The night, which had been dirty, cleared somewhat, and the bright crescent of the moon appeared above a heavy bank of clouds, as the cat, which had by dint of using its back as a lever at length got free from that cursed chest, licked its shapely limbs, and came up on deck. After its stifling prison, the air was simply delicious.

"Bob!" yelled the skipper suddenly.

"Ay, ay, sir!" said the look-out, in a startled voice.

"Did you mew?" inquired the skipper.

"Did I WOT, sir?" cried the astonished Bob.

"Mew," said the skipper sharply, "like a cat?"

"No, sir," said the offended seaman. "What 'ud I want to do that for?"

"I don't know what you want to for," said the skipper, looking round him uneasily. "There's some more rain coming, Bob."

"Ay, ay, sir," said Bob.

"Lot o' rain we've had this summer," said the skipper, in a meditative bawl.

"Ay, ay, sir," said Bob. "Sailing-ship on the port bow, sir."

The conversation dropped, the skipper, anxious to divert his thoughts, watching the dark mass of sail as it came plunging out of the darkness into the moonlight until it was abreast of his own craft. His eyes followed it as it passed his quarter, so that he saw not the stealthy approach of the cat which came from behind the companion, and sat down close by him. For over thirty hours the animal had been subjected to the grossest indignities at the hands of every man on board the ship except one. That one was the skipper, and there is no doubt but that its subsequent behaviour was a direct recognition of that fact. It rose to its feet, and crossing over to the unconscious skipper, rubbed its head affectionately and vigorously against his leg.

From simple causes great events do spring. The skipper sprang four yards, and let off a screech which was the subject of much comment on the barque which had just passed. When Bob, who came shuffling up at the double, reached him he was leaning against the side, incapable of speech, and shaking all over.

"Anything wrong, sir?" inquired the seaman anxiously, as he ran to the wheel.

The skipper pulled himself together a bit, and got closer to his companion.

"Believe me or not, Bob," he said at length, in trembling accents, "just as you please, but the ghost of that—cat, I mean the ghost of that poor affectionate animal which I drowned, and which I wish I hadn't, came and rubbed itself up against my leg."

"Which leg?" inquired Bob, who was ever careful about details.

"What the blazes does it matter which leg?" demanded the skipper, whose nerves were in a terrible state. "Ah, look—look there!"

The seaman followed his outstretched finger, and his heart failed him as he saw the cat, with its back arched, gingerly picking its way along the side of the vessel.

"I can't see nothing," he said doggedly.

"I don't suppose you can, Bob," said the skipper in a melancholy voice, as the cat vanished in the bows; "it's evidently only meant for me to see. What it means I don't know. I'm going down to turn in. I ain't fit for duty. You don't mind being left alone till the mate comes up, do you?"

"I ain't afraid," said Bob.

His superior officer disappeared below, and, shaking the sleepy mate, who protested strongly against the proceedings, narrated in trembling tones his horrible experiences.

"If I were you "—said the mate.

"Yes?" said the skipper, waiting a bit. Then he shook him again, roughly.

"What were you going to say?" he inquired.

"Say?" said the mate, rubbing his eyes. "Nothing."

"About the cat?" suggested the skipper.

"Cat?" said the mate, nestling lovingly down in the blankets again. "Wha' ca'—goo' ni'"—

Then the skipper drew the blankets from the mate's sleepy clutches, and, rolling him backwards and forwards in the bunk, patiently explained to him that he was very unwell, that he was going to have a drop of whiskey neat, and turn in, and that he, the mate, was to take the watch. From this moment the joke lost much of its savour for the mate.

"You can have a nip too, Dick," said the skipper, proffering him the whiskey, as the other sullenly dressed himself.

"It's all rot," said the mate, tossing the spirits down his throat, "and it's no use either; you can't run away from a ghost; it's just as likely to be in your bed as anywhere else. Good-night."

He left the skipper pondering over his last words, and dubiously eyeing the piece of furniture in question. Nor did he retire until he had subjected it to an analysis of the most searching description, and then, leaving the lamp burning, he sprang hastily in, and forgot his troubles in sleep.

It was day when he awoke, and went on deck to find a heavy sea running, and just sufficient sail set to keep the schooner's head before the wind as she bobbed about on the waters. An exclamation from the skipper, as a wave broke against the side and flung a cloud of spray over him, brought the mate's head round.

"Why, you ain't going to get up?" he said, in tones of insincere surprise.

"Why not?" inquired the other gruffly.

"You go and lay down agin," said the mate, "and have a cup o' nice hot tea an' some toast."

"Clear out," said the skipper, making a dash for the wheel, and reaching it as the wet deck suddenly changed its angle. "I know you didn't like being woke up, Dick; but I got the horrors last night. Go below and turn in."

"All right," said the mollified mate.

"You didn't see anything?" inquired the skipper, as he took the wheel from him.

"Nothing at all," said the other.

The skipper shook his head thoughtfully, then shook it again vigorously, as another shower-bath put its head over the side and saluted him.

"I wish I hadn't drowned that cat, Dick," he said.

"You won't see it again," said Dick, with the confidence of a man who had taken every possible precaution to render the prophecy a safe one.

He went below, leaving the skipper at the wheel idly watching the cook as he performed marvellous feats of jugglery, between the galley and the fo'c'sle, with the men's breakfast.

A little while later, leaving the wheel to Sam, he went below himself and had his own, talking freely, to the discomfort of the conscious-stricken cook, about his weird experiences of the night before.

"You won't see it no more, sir, I don't expect," he said faintly; "I b'leeve it come and rubbed itself up agin your leg to show it forgave you."

"Well, I hope it knows it's understood," said the other. "I don't want it to take any more trouble."

He finished the breakfast in silence, and then went on deck again. It was still blowing hard, and he went over to superintend the men who were attempting to lash together some empties which were rolling about in all directions amidships. A violent roll set them free again, and at the same time separated two chests in the fo'c'sle, which were standing one on top of the other. This enabled Satan, who was crouching in the lower one, half crazed with terror, to come flying madly up on deck and give his feelings full vent. Three times in full view of the horrified skipper he circled the deck at racing speed, and had just started on the fourth when a heavy packing-case, which had been temporarily set on end and abandoned by the men at his sudden appearance, fell over and caught him by the tail. Sam rushed to the rescue.

"Stop!" yelled the skipper.

"Won't I put it up, sir?" inquired Sam.

"Do you see what's beneath it?" said the skipper, in a husky voice.

"Beneath it, sir?" said Sam, whose ideas were in a whirl.

"The cat, can't you see the cat?" said the skipper, whose eyes had been riveted on the animal since its first appearance on deck.

Sam hesitated a moment, and then shook his head.

"The case has fallen on the cat," said the skipper. "I can see it distinctly."

He might have said heard it, too, for Satan was making frenzied appeals to his sympathetic friends for assistance.

"Let me put the case back, sir," said one of the men, "then p'raps the vision 'll disappear."

"No, stop where you are," said the skipper. "I can stand it better by daylight. It's the most wonderful and extraordinary thing I've ever seen. Do you mean to say you can't see anything, Sam?"

"I can see a case, sir," said Sam, speaking slowly and carefully," with a bit of rusty iron band sticking out from it. That's what you're mistaking for the cat, p'raps, sir."

"Can't you see anything, cook?" demanded the skipper.

"It may be fancy, sir," faltered the cook, lowering his eyes, "but it does seem to me as though I can see a little misty sort o' thing there. Ah, now it's gone."

"No, it ain't," said the skipper. "The ghost of Satan's sitting there. The case seems to have fallen on its tail. It appears to be howling something dreadful."

The men made a desperate effort to display the astonishment suitable to such a marvel, whilst Satan, who was trying all he knew to get his tail out, cursed freely. How long the superstitious captain of the Skylark would have let him remain there will never be known, for just then the mate came on deck and caught sight of it before he was quite aware of the part he was expected to play.

"Why the devil don't you lift the thing off the poor brute," he yelled, hurrying up towards the case.

"What, can YOU see it, Dick?" said the skipper impressively, laying his hand on his arm.

"SEE it?" retorted the mate. "D'ye think I'm blind. Listen to the poor brute. I should—Oh!"

He became conscious of the concentrated significant gaze of the crew. Five pairs of eyes speaking as one, all saying "idiot" plainly, the boy's eyes conveying an expression too great to be translated.

Turning, the skipper saw the bye-play, and a light slowly dawned upon him. But he wanted more, and he wheeled suddenly to the cook for the required illumination.

The cook said it was a lark. Then he corrected himself and said it wasn't a lark, then he corrected himself again and became incoherent.

Meantime the skipper eyed him stonily, while the mate released the cat and good-naturedly helped to straighten its tail.

It took fully five minutes of unwilling explanation before the skipper could grasp the situation. He did not appear to fairly understand it until he was shown the chest with the ventilated lid; then his countenance cleared, and, taking the unhappy Billy by the collar, he called sternly for a piece of rope.

By this statesmanlike handling of the subject a question of much delicacy and difficulty was solved, discipline was preserved, and a practical illustration of the perils of deceit afforded to a youngster who was at an age best suited to receive such impressions. That he should exhaust the resources of a youthful but powerful vocabulary upon the crew in general, and Sam in particular, was only to be expected.

They bore him no malice for it, but, when he showed signs of going beyond his years, held a hasty consultation, and then stopped his mouth with sixpence-halfpenny and a broken jack-knife.

A CASE OF DESERTION

The sun was just rising as the small tub-like steamer, or, to be more correct, steam-barge, the Bulldog, steamed past the sleeping town of Gravesend at a good six knots per hour.

There had been a little discussion on the way between her crew and the engineer, who, down in his grimy little engine-room, did his own stoking and everything else necessary. The crew, consisting of captain, mate, and boy, who were doing their first trip on a steamer, had been transferred at the last moment from their sailing-barge the Witch, and found to their discomfort that the engineer, who had not expected to sail so soon, was terribly and abusively drunk. Every moment he could spare from his engines he thrust the upper part of his body through the small hatchway, and rowed with his commander.

"Ahoy, bargee!" he shouted, popping up like a jack-in-the-box, after a brief cessation of hostilities.

"Don't take no notice of 'im," said the mate. "'E's got a bottle of brandy down there, an' he's 'alf mad."

"If I knew anything o' them blessed engines," growled the skipper, "I'd go and hit 'im over the head."

"But you don't," said the mate, "and neither do I, so you'd better keep quiet."

"You think you're a fine feller," continued the engineer, "standing up there an' playing with that little wheel. You think you're doing all the work. What's the boy doing? Send him down to stoke."

"Go down," said the skipper, grinning with fury, and the boy reluctantly obeyed.

"You think," said the engineer pathetically, after he had cuffed the boy's head and dropped him down below by the scruff of his neck, "you think because I've got a black face I'm not a man. There's many a hoily face 'ides a good 'art."

"I don't think nothing about it," grunted the skipper; "you do your work, and I'll do mine."

"Don't you give me none of your back answers," bellowed the engineer, "'cos I won't have 'em."

The skipper shrugged his shoulders and exchanged glances with his sympathetic mate. "Wait till I get 'im ashore," he murmured.

"The biler is wore out," said the engineer, re-appearing after a hasty dive below. "It may bust at any moment."

As though to confirm his words fearful sounds were heard proceeding from below.

"It's only the boy," said the mate, "he's scared—natural."

"I thought it was the biler," said the skipper, with a sigh of relief. "It was loud enough."

As he spoke the boy got his head out of the hatchway, and, rendered desperate with fear, fairly fought his way past the engineer and gained the deck.

"Very good," said the engineer, as he followed him on deck and staggered to the side. "I've had enough o' you lot."

"Hadn't you better go down to them engines?" shouted the skipper.

"Am I your SLAVE?" demanded the engineer tearfully. "Tell me that. Am I your slave?"

"Go down and do your work like a sensible man," was the reply.

At these words the engineer took umbrage at once, and, scowling fiercely, removed his greasy jacket and flung his cap on the deck. He then finished the brandy which he had brought up with him, and gazed owlishly at the Kentish shore.

"I'm going to have a wash," he said loudly, and, sitting down, removed his boots.

"Go down to the engines first," said the skipper, "and I'll send the boy to you with a bucket and some soap."

"Bucket!" replied the engineer scornfully, as he moved to the side. "I'm going to have a proper wash."

"Hold him!" roared the skipper suddenly. "Hold him!"

The mate, realising the situation, rushed to seize him, but the engineer, with a mad laugh, put his hands on the side and vaulted into the water. When he rose the steamer was twenty yards ahead.

"Go astarn!" yelled the mate.

"How can I go astarn when there's nobody at the engines?" shouted the skipper, as he hung on to the wheel and brought the boat's head sharply round. "Git a line ready."

The mate, with a coil of rope in his hand, rushed to the side, but his benevolent efforts were frustrated by the engineer, who, seeing the boat's head making straight for him, saved his life by an opportune dive. The steamer rushed by.

"Turn 'er agin!" screamed the mate.

The captain was already doing so, and in a remarkably short space of time the boat, which had described a complete circle, was making again for the engineer.

"Look out for the line!" shouted the mate warningly.

"I don't want your line," yelled the engineer. "I'm going ashore."

"Come aboard!" shouted the captain imploringly, as they swept past again. "We can't manage the engines."

"Put her round again," said the mate. "I'll go for him with the boat. Haul her in, boy."

The boat, which was dragging astern, was hauled close, and the mate tumbled into her, followed by the boy, just as the captain was in the middle of another circle? to the intense indignation of a crowd of shipping, large and small, which was trying to get by.

"Ahoy!" yelled the master of a tug which was towing a large ship." Take that steam roundabout out of the way. What the thunder are you doing?"

"Picking up my engineer," replied the captain, as he steamed right across the other's bows, and nearly ran down a sailing-barge, the skipper of which, a Salvation Army man, was nobly fighting with his feelings.

"Why don't you stop?" he yelled.

"'Cos I can't," wailed the skipper of the Bulldog, as he threaded his way between a huge steamer and a schooner, who, in avoiding him, were getting up a little collision on their own account.

"Ahoy, Bulldog! Ahoy!" called the mate. "Stand by to pick us up. We've got him."

The skipper smiled in an agonised fashion as he shot past, hotly pursued by his boat. The feeling on board the other craft as they got out of the way of the Bulldog, and nearly ran down her boat, and then, in avoiding that, nearly ran down something else, cannot be put into plain English, but several captains ventured into the domains of the ornamental with marked success.

"Shut off steam!" yelled the engineer, as the Bulldog went by again. "Draw the fires, then."

"Who's going to steer while I do it?" bellowed the skipper, as he left the wheel for a few seconds to try and get a line to throw them.

By this time the commotion in the river was frightful, and the captain's steering, as he went on his round again, something marvellous to behold. A strange lack of sympathy on the part of brother captains added to his troubles. Every craft he passed had something to say to him, busy as they were, and the remarks were as monotonous as they were insulting. At last, just as he was resolving to run his boat straight down the river until he came to a halt for want of steam, the mate caught the rope he flung, and the Bulldog went down the river with her boat made fast to her stern.

"Come aboard, you—you lunatic!" he shouted.

"Not afore I knows 'ow I stand," said the engineer, who was now beautifully sober, and in full possession of a somewhat acute intellect.

"What do you mean?" demanded the skipper.

"I don't come aboard," shouted the engineer, "until you and the mate and the bye all swear as you won't say nothing about this little game."

"I'll report you the moment I get ashore," roared the skipper. "I'll give you in charge for desertion. I'll"—

With a supreme gesture the engineer prepared to dive, but the watchful mate fell on his neck and tripped him over a seat.

"Come aboard!" cried the skipper, aghast at such determination. "Come aboard, and I'll give you a licking when we get ashore instead."

"Honour bright?" inquired the engineer.

"Honour bright," chorused the three.

The engineer, with all the honours of war, came on board, and, after remarking that he felt chilly bathing on an empty stomach, went down below and began to stoke. In the course of the voyage he said that it was worth while making such a fool of himself if only to see the skipper's beautiful steering, warmly asseverating that there was not another man on the river that could have done it. Before this insidious flattery the skipper's wrath melted like snow before the sun, and by the time they reached port he would as soon have thought of hitting his own father as his smooth-tongued engineer.

A CHANGE OF TREATMENT

"Yes, I've sailed under some 'cute skippers in my time," said the night-watchman; "them that go down in big ships see the wonders o' the deep, you know," he added with a sudden chuckle, "but the one I'm going to tell you about ought never to have been trusted out without 'is ma. A good many o' my skippers had fads, but this one was the worst I ever sailed under.

"It's some few years ago now; I'd shipped on his barque, the John Elliott, as slow-going an old tub as ever I was aboard of, when I wasn't in quite a fit an' proper state to know what I was doing, an' I hadn't been in her two days afore I found out his 'obby through overhearing a few remarks made by the second mate, who came up from dinner in a hurry to make 'em. 'I don't mind saws an' knives hung round the cabin,' he ses to the fust mate, 'but when a chap has a 'uman 'and alongside 'is plate, studying it while folks is at their food, it's more than a Christian man can stand.'

"'That's nothing,' ses the fust mate, who had sailed with the barque afore. 'He's half crazy on doctoring. We nearly had a mutiny aboard once owing to his wanting to hold a post-mortem on a man what fell from the mast-head. Wanted to see what the poor feller died of.'

"'I call it unwholesome,' ses the second mate very savage.' He offered me a pill at breakfast the size of a small marble; quite put me off my feed, it did.'

"Of course, the skipper's fad soon got known for'ard. But I didn't think much about it, till one day I seed old Dan'l Dennis sitting on a locker reading. Every now and then he'd shut the book, an' look up, closing 'is eyes, an' moving his lips like a hen drinking, an' then look down at the book again.

"'Why, Dan,' I ses, 'what's up? you ain't larning lessons at your time o' life?'

"'Yes, I am,' ses Dan very soft. 'You might hear me say it, it's this one about heart disease.'

"He hands over the book, which was stuck full o' all kinds o' diseases, and winks at me 'ard.

"'Picked it up on a book-stall,' he ses; then he shut 'is eyes an' said his piece wonderful. It made me quite queer to listen to 'im. 'That's how I feel,' ses he, when he'd finished. 'Just strength enough to get to bed. Lend a hand, Bill, an' go an' fetch the doctor.'

"Then I see his little game, but I wasn't going to run any risks, so I just mentioned, permiscous like, to the cook as old Dan seemed rather queer, an' went back an' tried to borrer the book, being always fond of reading. Old Dan pretended he was too ill to hear what I was saying, an' afore I could take it away from him, the skipper comes hurrying down with a bag in his 'and.

"'What's the matter, my man?' ses he, 'what's the matter?'

"'I'm all right, sir,' ses old Dan, "cept that I've been swoonding away a little.'

"'Tell me exactly how you feel,' ses the skipper, feeling his pulse.

"Then old Dan said his piece over to him, an' the skipper shook his head an' looked very solemn.

"'How long have you been like this?' he ses.

"'Four or five years, sir,' ses Dan. 'It ain't nothing serious, sir, is it?'

"'You lie quite still,' ses the skipper, putting a little trumpet thing to his chest an' then listening. 'Um! there's serious mischief here I'm afraid, the prognotice is very bad.'

"'Prog what, sir?' ses Dan, staring.

"'Prognotice,' ses the skipper, at least I think that's the word he said. 'You keep perfectly still, an' I'll go an' mix you up a draught, and tell the cook to get some strong beef-tea on.'

"Well, the skipper 'ad no sooner gone, than Cornish Harry, a great big lumbering chap o' six feet two, goes up to old Dan, an' he ses, 'Gimme that book.'

"'Go away,' says Dan, 'don't come worrying 'ere; you 'eard the skipper say how bad my prognotice was.'

"'You lend me the book,' ses Harry, ketching hold of him, 'or else I'll bang you first, and split to the skipper arterwards. I believe I'm a bit consumptive. Anyway, I'm going to see.'

"He dragged the book away from the old man, and began to study. There was so many complaints in it he was almost tempted to have something else instead of consumption, but he decided on that at last, an' he got a cough what worried the fo'c'sle all night long, an' the next day, when the skipper came down to see Dan, he could 'ardly 'ear hisself speak.

"'That's a nasty cough you've got, my man,' ses he, looking at Harry.

"'Oh, it's nothing, sir,' ses Harry, careless like. 'I've 'ad it for months now off and on. I think it's perspiring so of a night does it."

"'What?' ses the skipper. 'Do you perspire of a night?'

"'Dredful,' ses Harry. 'You could wring the clo'es out. I s'pose it's healthy for me, ain't it, sir?'

"'Undo your shirt,' ses the skipper, going over to him, an' sticking the trumpet agin him. 'Now take a deep breath. Don't cough.'

"'I can't help it, sir,' ses Harry, 'it will come. Seems to tear me to pieces.'

"'You get to bed at once," says the skipper, taking away the trumpet, an' shaking his 'ed. 'It's a fortunate thing for you, my lad, you're in skilled hands. With care, I believe I can pull you round. How does that medicine suit you, Dan?'

"'Beautiful, sir,' says Dan. 'It's wonderful soothing, I slep' like a new-born babe arter it.'

"'I'll send you some more,' ses the skipper. 'You're not to get up mind, either of you.'

"'All right, sir,' ses the two in very faint voices, an' the skipper went away arter telling us to be careful not to make a noise.

"We all thought it a fine joke at first, but the airs them two chaps give themselves was something sickening. Being in bed all day, they was naturally wakeful of a night, and they used to call across the fo'c'sle inquiring arter each other's healths, an' waking us other chaps up. An' they'd swop beef-tea an' jellies with each other, an' Dan 'ud try an' coax a little port wine out o' Harry, which he 'ad to make blood with, but Harry 'ud say he hadn't made enough that day, an! he'd drink to the better health of old Dan's prognotice, an' smack his lips until it drove us a'most crazy to 'ear him.

"Arter these chaps had been ill two days, the other fellers began to put their heads together, being maddened by the smell o' beef-tea an' the like, an' said they was going to be ill too, and both the invalids got into a fearful state of excitement.

"'You'll only spoil it for all of us,' ses Harry, 'and you don't know what to have without the book.'

"'It's all very well doing your work as well as our own,' ses one of the men. 'It's our turn now. It's time you two got well.'

"'WELL? ses Harry, 'well? Why you silly iggernerant chaps, we shan't never get well, people with our complaints never do. You ought to know that.'

"'Well, I shall split, 'ses one of them. "'You do!' ses Harry, 'you do, an' I'll put a 'ed on you that all the port wine and jellies in the world wouldn't cure. 'Sides, don't you think the skipper knows what's the matter with us?'

"'Afore the other chap could reply, the skipper hisself comes down, accompanied by the fust mate, with a look on his face which made Harry give the deepest and hollowest cough he'd ever done.

"'What they reely want,' ses the skipper, turning to the mate, 'is keerful nussing.'

"'I wish you'd let me nuss 'em,' ses the fust mate, 'only ten minutes, I'd put 'em both on their legs, an' running for their lives into the bargain, in ten minutes.'

"'Hold your tongue, sir,' ses the skipper; 'what you say is unfeeling, besides being an insult to me. Do you think I studied medicine all these years without knowing when a man's ill?'

"The fust mate growled something and went on deck, and the skipper started examining of 'em again. He said they was wonderfully patient lying in bed so long, an' he had 'em wrapped up in bedclo'es and carried on deck, so as the pure air could have a go at 'em. WE had to do the carrying, an' there they sat, breathing the pure air, and looking at the fust mate out of the corners of their eyes. If they wanted anything from below one of us had to go an' fetch it, an' by the time they was taken down to bed again, we all resolved to be took ill too.

"Only two of 'em did it though, for Harry, who was a powerful, ugly-tempered chap, swore he'd do all sorts o' dreadful things to us if we didn't keep well and hearty, an' all 'cept these two did. One of 'em, Mike Rafferty, laid up with a swelling on his ribs, which I knew myself he 'ad 'ad for fifteen years, and the other chap had paralysis. I never saw a man so reely happy as the skipper was. He was up an down with his medicines and his instruments all day long, and used to make notes of the cases in a big pocket-book, and read 'em to the second mate at mealtimes.

"The fo'c'sle had been turned into hospital about a week, an' I was on deck doing some odd job or the other, when the cook comes up to me pulling a face as long as a fiddle.

"'Nother invalid,' ses he; 'fust mate's gone stark, staring mad!'

"'Mad?' ses I.

"'Yes,' ses he. 'He's got a big basin in the galley, an' he's laughing like a hyener an' mixing bilge-water an' ink, an' paraffin an' butter an' soap an' all sorts o' things up together. The smell's enough to kill a man; I've had to come away.'

"Curious-like, I jest walked up to the galley an' puts my 'ed in, an' there was the mate as the cook said, smiling all over his face, and ladling some thick sticky stuff into a stone bottle.

"'How's the pore sufferers, sir?' ses he, stepping out of the galley jest as the skipper was going by.

"'They're very bad; but I hope for the best," ses the skipper, looking at him hard. 'I'm glad to see you've turned a bit more feeling.'

"'Yes, sir,' ses the mate. 'I didn't think so at fust, but I can see now them chaps is all very ill. You'll s'cuse me saying it, but I don't quite approve of your treatment.'

"I thought the skipper would ha' bust.

"'My treatment?' ses he. 'My treatment? What do you know about it ?'

"'You're treating 'em wrong, sir,' ses the mate. 'I have here' (patting the jar) 'a remedy which 'ud cure them all if you'd only let me try it.'

"'Pooh!' ses the skipper. 'One medicine cure all diseases! The old story. What is it? Where'd you get it from?' ses he.

"'I brought the ingredients aboard with me,' ses the mate. 'It's a wonderful medicine discovered by my grandmother, an' if I might only try it I'd thoroughly cure them pore chaps.'

"'Rubbish!' ses the skipper.

"'Very well, sir,' ses the mate, shrugging his shoulders. "O' course, if you won't let me you won't. Still I tell you, if you'd let me try I'd cure 'em all in two days. That's a fair challenge.'

"Well, they talked, and talked, and talked, until at last the skipper give way and went down below with the mate, and told the chaps they was to take the new medicine for two days, jest to prove the mate was wrong.

"'Let pore old Dan try it first, sir,' ses Harry, starting up, an' sniffing as the mate took the cork out; 'he's been awful bad since you've been away.'

"'Harry's worse than I am, sir,' ses Dan; 'it's only his kind heart that makes him say that.'

"'It don't matter which is fust,' ses the mate, filling a tablespoon with it, 'there's plenty for all. Now, Harry.'

"'Take it,' ses the skipper.

"Harry took it, an' the fuss he made you'd ha' thought he was swallering a football. It stuck all round his mouth, and he carried on so dredful that the other invalids was half sick afore it came to them.

"By the time the other three 'ad 'ad theirs it was as good as a pantermime, an' the mate corked the bottle up, and went an' sat down on a locker while they tried to rinse their mouths out with the luxuries which had been given 'em.

"'How do you feel?' ses the skipper.

"'I'm dying,' ses Dan.

"'So'm I,' ses Harry; 'I b'leeve the mate's pisoned us."

"The skipper looks over at the mate very stern an' shakes his 'ed slowly.

"'It's all right,' ses the mate. 'It's always like that the first dozen or so doses.'

"'Dozen or so doses!' ses old Dan, in a far-away voice.

"'It has to be taken every twenty minutes,' ses the mate, pulling out his pipe and lighting it; an' the four men groaned all together.

"'I can't allow it,' ses the skipper, 'I can't allow it. Men's lives mustn't be sacrificed for an experiment.'

"''T ain't a experiment,' ses the mate very indignant, 'it's an old family medicine.'

"'Well, they shan't have any more,' ses the skipper firmly.

"'Look here,' ses the mate. 'If I kill any one o' these men I'll give you twenty pound. Honour bright, I will.'

"'Make it twenty-five,' ses the skipper, considering.

"'Very good,' ses the mate. 'Twenty-five; I can't say no fairer than that, can I? It's about time for another dose now.'

"He gave 'em another tablespoonful all round as the skipper left, an' the chaps what wasn't invalids nearly bust with joy. He wouldn't let 'em have anything to take the taste out, 'cos he said it didn't give the medicine a chance, an' he told us other chaps to remove the temptation, an' you bet we did.

"After the fifth dose, the invalids began to get desperate, an' when they heard they'd got to be woke up every twenty minutes through the night to take the stuff, they sort o' give up. Old Dan said he felt a gentle glow stealing over him and strengthening him, and Harry said that it felt like a healing balm to his lungs. All of 'em agreed it was a wonderful sort o' medicine, an' arter the sixth dose the man with paralysis dashed up on deck, and ran up the rigging like a cat. He sat there for hours spitting, an' swore he'd brain anybody who interrupted him, an' arter a little while Mike Rafferty went up and j'ined him, an' it the fust mate's ears didn't burn by reason of the things them two pore sufferers said about 'im, they ought to.

"They was all doing full work next day, an' though, o'course, the skipper saw how he'd been done, he didn't allude to it. Not in words, that is; but when a man tries to make four chaps do the work of eight, an' hits 'em when they don't, it's a easy job to see where the shoe pinches."

A CIRCULAR TOUR

Illness? said the night watchman, slowly. Yes, sailormen get ill sometimes, but not 'aving the time for it that other people have, and there being no doctors at sea, they soon pick up agin. Ashore, if a man's ill he goes to a horse-pittle and 'as a nice nurse to wait on 'im; at sea the mate comes down and tells 'im that there is nothing the matter with 'im, and asks 'im if he ain't ashamed of 'imself. The only mate I ever knew that showed any feeling was one who 'ad been a doctor and 'ad gone to sea to better 'imself. He didn't believe in medicine; his idea was to cut things out, and he was so kind and tender, and so fond of 'is little box of knives and saws, that you wouldn't ha' thought anybody could 'ave had the 'art to say "no" to him. But they did. I remember 'im getting up at four o'clock one morning to cut a man's leg off, and at ha'-past three the chap was sitting up aloft with four pairs o' trousers on and a belaying-pin in his 'and.

One chap I knew, Joe Summers by name, got so sick o' work one v'y'ge that he went mad. Not dangerous mad, mind you. Just silly. One thing he did was to pretend that the skipper was 'is little boy, and foller 'im up unbeknown and pat his 'ead. At last, to pacify him, the old man pretended that he was 'is little boy, and a precious handful of a boy he was too, I can tell you. Fust of all he showed 'is father 'ow they wrestled at school, and arter that he showed 'im 'ow he 'arf killed another boy in fifteen rounds. Leastways he was going to, but arter seven rounds Joe's madness left 'im all of a sudden and he was as right as ever he was.

Sailormen are more frequent ill ashore than at sea; they've got more time for it, I s'pose. Old Sam Small, a man you may remember by name as a pal o' mine, got ill once, and, like most 'ealthy men who get a little something the matter with 'em, he made sure 'e was dying. He was sharing a bedroom with Ginger Dick and Peter Russet at the time, and early one morning he woke up groaning with a chill or something which he couldn't account for, but which Ginger thought might ha' been partly caused through 'im sleeping in the fireplace.

"Is that you, Sam?" ses Ginger, waking up with the noise and rubbing his eyes. "Wot's the matter?"

"I'm dying," ses Sam, with another awful groan. "Good-by, Ginger."

"Goo'-by," ses Ginger, turning over and falling fast asleep agin.

Old Sam picked 'imself up arter two or three tries, and then he staggered over to Peter Russet's bed and sat on the foot of it, groaning, until Peter woke up very cross and tried to push 'im off with his feet.

"I'm dying, Peter," ses Sam, and 'e rolled over and buried his face in the bed-clo'es and kicked. Peter Russet, who was a bit scared, sat up in bed and called for Ginger, and arter he 'ad called pretty near a dozen times Ginger 'arf woke up and asked 'im wot was the matter.

"Poor old Sam's dying," ses Peter.

"I know," ses Ginger, laying down and cuddling into the piller agin. "He told me just now. I've bid 'im good-by."

Peter Russet asked 'im where his 'art was, but Ginger was asleep agin. Then Peter sat up in bed and tried to comfort Sam, and listened while 'e told 'im wot it felt like to die. How 'e was 'ot and cold all over, burning and shivering, with pains in his inside that he couldn't describe if 'e tried.

"It'll soon be over, Sam," ses Peter, kindly, "and all your troubles will be at an end. While me and Ginger are knocking about at sea trying to earn a crust o' bread to keep ourselves alive, you'll be quiet and at peace."

Sam groaned. "I don't like being too quiet," he ses. "I was always one for a bit o' fun—innercent fun."

Peter coughed.

"You and Ginger 'av been good pals," ses Sam; "it's hard to go and leave you."

"We've all got to go some time or other, Sam," ses Peter, soothing-like. "It's a wonder to me, with your habits, that you've lasted as long as you 'ave."

"My habits?" ses Sam, sitting up all of a sudden. "Why, you monkey-faced son of a sea-cook, for two pins I'd chuck you out of the winder."

"Don't talk like that on your death-bed," ses Peter, very shocked.

Sam was going to answer 'im sharp agin, but just then 'e got a pain which made 'im roll about on the bed and groan to such an extent that Ginger woke up agin and got out o' bed.

"Pore old Sam!" he ses, walking across the room and looking at 'im. "'Ave you got any pain anywhere?"

"Pain?" ses Sam. "Pain? I'm a mask o' pains all over."

Ginger and Peter looked at 'im and shook their 'eds, and then they went a little way off and talked about 'im in whispers.

"He looks 'arf dead now," ses Peter, coming back and staring at 'im. "Let's take 'is clothes off, Ginger; it's more decent to die with 'em off."

"I think I'll 'ave a doctor," ses Sam, in a faint voice.

"You're past doctors, Sam," ses Ginger, in a kind voice.

"Better 'ave your last moments in peace," ses Peter, "and keep your money in your trouser-pockets."

"You go and fetch a doctor, you murderers," ses Sam, groaning, as Peter started to undress 'im. "Go on, else I'll haunt you with my ghost."

Ginger tried to talk to 'im about the sin o' wasting money, but it was all no good, and arter telling Peter wot to do in case Sam died afore he come back, he went off. He was gone about 'arf an hour, and then he come back with a sandy-'aired young man with red eyelids and a black bag.

"Am I dying, sir?" ses Sam, arter the doctor 'ad listened to his lungs and his 'art and prodded 'im all over.

"We're all dying," ses the doctor, "only some of us'll go sooner than others."

"Will he last the day, sir?" ses Ginger.

The doctor looked at Sam agin, and Sam held 'is breath while 'e waited for him to answer. "Yes," ses the doctor at last, "if he does just wot I tell him and takes the medicine I send 'im."

He wasn't in the room 'arf an hour altogether, and he charged pore Sam a shilling; but wot 'urt Sam even more than that was to hear 'im go off downstairs whistling as cheerful as if there wasn't a dying man within a 'undred miles.

Peter and Ginger Dick took turns to be with Sam that morning, but in the arternoon the landlady's mother, an old lady who was almost as fat as Sam 'imself, came up to look arter 'im a bit. She sat on a chair by the side of 'is bed and tried to amuse 'im by telling 'im of all the death-beds she'd been at, and partikler of one man, the living image of Sam, who passed away in his sleep. It was past ten o'clock when Peter and Ginger came 'ome, but they found pore Sam still awake and sitting up in bed holding 'is eyes open with his fingers.

Sam had another shilling's-worth the next day, and 'is medicine was changed for the worse. If anything he seemed a trifle better, but the landlady's mother, wot came up to nurse 'im agin, said it was a bad sign, and that people often brightened up just afore the end. She asked 'im whether 'e'd got a fancy for any partikler spot to be buried in, and, talking about wot a lot o' people 'ad been buried alive, said she'd ask the doctor to cut Sam's 'ead off to prevent mistakes. She got quite annoyed with Sam for saying, supposing there was a mistake and he came round in the middle of it, how'd he feel? and said there was no satisfying some people, do wot you would.

At the end o' six days Sam was still alive and losing a shilling a day, to say nothing of buying 'is own beef-tea and such-like. Ginger said it was fair highway robbery, and tried to persuade Sam to go to a 'orsepittle, where he'd 'ave lovely nurses to wait on 'im hand and foot, and wouldn't keep 'is best friends awake of a night making 'orrible noises.

Sam didn't take kindly to the idea at fust, but as the doctor forbid 'im to get up, although he felt much better, and his money was wasting away, he gave way at last, and at seven o'clock one evening he sent Ginger off to fetch a cab to take 'im to the London Horsepittle. Sam said something about putting 'is clothes on, but Peter Russet said the horsepittle would be more likely to take him in if he went in the blanket and counterpane, and at last Sam gave way. Ginger and Peter helped 'im downstairs, and the cabman laid hold o' one end o' the blanket as they got to the street-door, under the idea that he was helping, and very near gave Sam another chill.

"Keep your hair on," he ses, as Sam started on 'im. "It'll be three-and-six for the fare, and I'll take the money now."

"You'll 'ave it when you get there," ses Ginger.

"I'll 'ave it now," ses the cabman. "I 'ad a fare die on the way once afore."

Ginger—who was minding Sam's money for 'im because there wasn't a pocket in the counterpane— paid 'im, and the cab started. It jolted and rattled over the stones, but Sam said the air was doing 'im good. He kept 'is pluck up until they got close to the horsepittle, and then 'e got nervous. And 'e got more nervous when the cabman got down off 'is box and put his 'ed in at the winder and spoke to 'im.

"'Ave you got any partikler fancy for the London Horsepittle?" he ses.

"No," ses Sam. "Why?"

"Well, I s'pose it don't matter, if wot your mate ses is true—that you're dying," ses the cabman.

"Wot d'ye mean?" says Sam.

"Nothing," ses the cabman; "only, fust and last, I s'pose I've driven five 'undred people to that 'orsepittle, and only one ever came out agin—and he was smuggled out in a bread-basket."

Sam's flesh began to creep all over.

"It's a pity they don't 'ave the same rules as Charing Cross Horsepittle," ses the cabman. "The doctors 'ave five pounds apiece for every patient that gets well there, and the consequence is they ain't 'ad the blinds down for over five months."

"Drive me there," ses Sam.

"It's a long way," ses the cabman, shaking his 'ed, "and it 'ud cost you another 'arf dollar. S'pose you give the London a try?"

"You drive to Charing Cross," ses Sam, telling Ginger to give 'im the 'arf-dollar. "And look sharp; these things ain't as warm as they might be."

The cabman turned his 'orse round and set off agin, singing. The cab stopped once or twice for a little while, and then it stopped for quite a long time, and the cabman climbed down off 'is box and came to the winder agin.

"I'm sorry, mate," he ses, "but did you see me speak to that party just now?"

"The one you flicked with your whip?" ses Ginger.

"No; he was speaking to me," ses the cabman. "The last one, I mean."

"Wot about it?" ses Peter.

"He's the under-porter at the horsepittle," ses the cabman, spitting; "and he tells me that every bed is bung full, and two patients apiece in some of 'em."

"I don't mind sleeping two in a bed," ses Sam, who was very tired and cold.

"No," ses the cabman, looking at 'im; "but wot about the other one?"

"Well, what's to be done?" ses Peter.

"You might go to Guy's," ses the cabman; "that's as good as Charing Cross."

"I b'lieve you're telling a pack o' lies," ses Ginger.

"Come out o' my cab," ses the cabman, very fierce. "Come on, all of you. Out you get."

Ginger and Peter was for getting out, but Sam wouldn't 'ear of it. It was bad enough being wrapped up in a blanket in a cab, without being turned out in 'is bare feet on the pavement, and at last Ginger apologized to the cabman by saying 'e supposed if he was a liar he couldn't 'elp it. The cabman collected three shillings more to go to Guy's 'orsepittle, and, arter a few words with Ginger, climbed up on 'is box and drove off agin.

They were all rather tired of the cab by this time, and, going over Waterloo Bridge, Ginger began to feel uncommon thirsty, and, leaning out of the winder, he told the cabman to pull up for a drink. He was so long about it that Ginger began to think he was bearing malice, but just as he was going to tell 'im agin, the cab pulled up in a quiet little street opposite a small pub. Ginger Dick and Peter went in and 'ad something and brought one out for Sam. They 'ad another arter that, and Ginger, getting 'is good temper back agin, asked the cabman to 'ave one.

"Look lively about it, Ginger," ses Sam, very sharp. "You forget 'ow ill I am."

Ginger said they wouldn't be two seconds, and, the cabman calling a boy to mind his 'orse, they went inside. It was a quiet little place, but very cosey, and Sam, peeping out of the winder, could see all three of 'em leaning against the bar and making themselves comfortable. Twice he made the boy go in to hurry them up, and all the notice they took was to go on at the boy for leaving the horse.

Pore old Sam sat there hugging 'imself in the bed-clo'es, and getting wilder and wilder. He couldn't get out of the cab, and 'e couldn't call to them for fear of people coming up and staring at 'im. Ginger, smiling all over with 'appiness, had got a big cigar on and was pretending to pinch the barmaid's flowers, and Peter and the cabman was talking to some other chaps there. The only change Sam 'ad was when the boy walked the 'orse up and down the road.

He sat there for an hour and then 'e sent the boy in agin. This time the cabman lost 'is temper, and, arter chasing the boy up the road, gave a young feller twopence to take 'is place and promised 'im another twopence when he came out. Sam tried to get a word with 'im as 'e passed, but he wouldn't listen, and it was pretty near 'arf an hour later afore they all came out, talking and laughing.

"Now for the 'orsepittle," ses Ginger, opening the door. "Come on, Peter; don't keep pore old Sam waiting all night."

"'Arf a tic," ses the cabman, "'arf a tic; there's five shillings for waiting, fust."

"Wot?" ses Ginger, staring at 'im. "Arter giving you all them drinks?"

"Five shillings," ses the cabman; "two hours' waiting at half a crown an hour. That's the proper charge."

Ginger thought 'e was joking at fust, and when he found 'e wasn't he called 'im all the names he could think of, while Peter Russet stood by smiling and trying to think where 'e was and wot it was all about.

"Pay 'im the five bob, Ginger, and 'ave done with it," ses pore Sam, at last. "I shall never get to the horsepittle at this rate."

"Cert'inly not," ses Ginger, "not if we stay 'ere all night."

"Pay 'im the five bob," ses Sam, raising 'is voice; "it's my money."

"You keep quiet," ses Ginger, "and speak when your spoke to. Get inside, Peter."

Peter, wot was standing by blinking and smiling, misunderstood 'im, and went back inside the pub. Ginger went arter 'im to fetch 'im back, and hearing a noise turned round and saw the cabman pulling Sam out o' the cab. He was just in time to shove 'im back agin, and for the next two or three minutes 'im and the cabman was 'ard at it. Sam was too busy holding 'is clothes on to do much, and twice the cabman got 'im 'arf out, and twice Ginger got him back agin and bumped 'im back in 'is seat and shut the door. Then they both stopped and took breath.

"We'll see which gets tired fust," ses Ginger. "Hold the door inside, Sam."

The cabman looked at 'im, and then 'e climbed up on to 'is seat and, just as Ginger ran back for Peter Russet, drove off at full speed.

Pore Sam leaned back in 'is seat panting and trying to wrap 'imself up better in the counterpane, which 'ad got torn in the struggle. They went through street arter street, and 'e was just thinking of a nice warm bed and a kind nurse listening to all 'is troubles when 'e found they was going over London Bridge.

"You've passed it," he ses, putting his 'ead out of the winder.

The cabman took no notice, and afore Sam could think wot to make of it they was in the Whitechapel Road, and arter that, although Sam kept putting his 'ead out of the winder and asking 'im questions, they kept going through a lot o' little back streets until 'e began to think the cabman 'ad lost 'is way. They stopped at last in a dark little road, in front of a brick wall, and then the cabman got down and opened a door and led his 'orse and cab into a yard.

"Do you call this Guy's Horsepittle?" ses Sam.

"Hullo!" ses the cabman. "Why, I thought I put you out o' my cab once."

"I'll give you five minutes to drive me to the 'orsepittle," ses Sam. "Arter that I shall go for the police."

"All right," ses the cabman, taking his 'orse out and leading it into a stable. "Mind you don't catch cold."

He lighted a lantern and began to look arter the 'orse, and pore Sam sat there getting colder and colder and wondering wot 'e was going to do.

"I shall give you in charge for kidnapping me," he calls out very loud.

"Kidnapping?" ses the cabman. "Who do you think wants to kidnap you? The gate's open, and you can go as soon as you like."

Sam climbed out of the cab, and holding up the counterpane walked across the yard in 'is bare feet to the stable. "Well, will you drive me 'ome?" he ses.

"Cert'inly not," ses the cabman; "I'm going 'ome myself now. It's time you went, 'cos I'm going to lock up."

"'Ow can I go like this?" ses Sam, bursting with passion. "Ain't you got any sense?"

"Well, wot are you going to do?" ses the cabman, picking 'is teeth with a bit o' straw.

"Wot would you do if you was me?" ses Sam, calming down a bit and trying to speak civil.

"Well, if I was you," said the cabman, speaking very slow, "I should be more perlite to begin with; you accused me just now—me, a 'ard-working man—o' kidnapping you."

"It was only my fun," ses Sam, very quick.

"I ain't kidnapping you, am I?" ses the cabman.

"Cert'inly not," ses Sam.

"Well, then," ses the cabman, "if I was you I should pay 'arf a crown for a night's lodging in this nice warm stable, and in the morning I should ask the man it belongs to—that's me—to go up to my lodging with a letter, asking for a suit o' clothes and eleven-and-six."

"Eleven-and-six?" ses Sam, staring.

"Five bob for two hours' wait," ses the cabman, "four shillings for the drive here, and 'arf a crown for the stable. That's fair, ain't it?"

Sam said it was—as soon as he was able to speak—and then the cabman gave 'im a truss of straw to lay on and a rug to cover 'im up with.

And then, calling 'imself a fool for being so tender-'earted, he left Sam the lantern, and locked the stable-door and went off.

It seemed like a 'orrid dream to Sam, and the only thing that comforted 'im was the fact that he felt much better. His illness seemed to 'ave gone, and arter hunting round the stable to see whether 'e could find anything to eat, 'e pulled the rug over him and went to sleep.

He was woke up at six o'clock in the morning by the cabman opening the door. There was a lovely smell o' hot tea from a tin he 'ad in one 'and, and a lovelier smell still from a plate o' bread and butter and bloaters in the other. Sam sniffed so 'ard that at last the cabman noticed it, and asked 'im whether he 'ad got a cold. When Sam explained he seemed to think a minute or two, and then 'e said that it was 'is breakfast, but Sam could 'ave it if 'e liked to make up the money to a pound.

"Take it or leave it," he ses, as Sam began to grumble.

Poor Sam was so 'ungry he took it, and it done him good. By the time he 'ad eaten it he felt as right as ninepence, and 'e took such a dislike to the cabman 'e could hardly be civil to 'im. And when the cabman spoke about the letter to Ginger Dick he spoke up and tried to bate 'im down to seven-and-six.

"You write that letter for a pound," ses the cabman, looking at 'im very fierce, "or else you can walk 'ome in your counterpane, with 'arf the boys in London follering you and trying to pull it off."

Sam rose 'im to seventeen-and-six, but it was all no good, and at last 'e wrote a letter to Ginger Dick, telling 'im to give the cabman a suit of clothes and a pound.

"And look sharp about it," he ses. "I shall expect 'em in 'arf an hour."

"You'll 'ave 'em, if you're lucky, when I come back to change 'orses at four o'clock," ses the cabman. "D'ye think I've got nothing to do but fuss about arter you?"

"Why not drive me back in the cab?" ses Sam.

"'Cos I wasn't born yesterday," ses the cabman.

He winked at Sam, and then, whistling very cheerful, took his 'orse out and put it in the cab. He was so good-tempered that 'e got quite playful, and Sam 'ad to tell him that when 'e wanted to 'ave his legs tickled with a straw he'd let 'im know.

Some people can't take a 'int, and, as the cabman wouldn't be'ave 'imself, Sam walked into a shed that was handy and pulled the door to, and he stayed there until he 'eard 'im go back to the stable for 'is rug. It was only a yard or two from the shed to the cab, and, 'ardly thinking wot he was doing, Sam nipped out and got into it and sat huddled up on the floor.

He sat there holding 'is breath and not daring to move until the cabman 'ad shut the gate and was driving off up the road, and then 'e got up on the seat and lolled back out of sight. The shops were just opening, the sun was shining, and Sam felt so well that 'e was thankful that 'e hadn't got to the horsepittle arter all.

The cab was going very slow, and two or three times the cabman 'arf pulled up and waved his whip at people wot he thought wanted a cab, but at last an old lady and gentleman, standing on the edge of the curb with a big bag, held up their 'ands to 'im. The cab pulled in to the curb, and the old gentleman 'ad just got hold of the door and was trying to open it when he caught sight of Sam.

"Why, you've got a fare," he ses.

"No, sir," ses the cabman.

"But I say you 'ave," ses the old gentleman.

The cabman climbed down off 'is box and looked in at the winder, and for over two minutes he couldn't speak a word. He just stood there looking at Sam and getting purpler and purpler about the face.

"Drive on, cabby," ses Sam, "Wot are you stopping for?"

The cabman tried to tell 'im, but just then a policeman came walking up to see wot was the matter, and 'e got on the box agin and drove off. Cabmen love policemen just about as much as cats love dogs, and he drove down two streets afore he stopped and got down agin to finish 'is remarks.

"Not so much talk, cabman," ses Sam, who was beginning to enjoy 'imself, "else I shall call the police."

"Are you coming out o' my cab?" ses the cabman, "or 'ave I got to put you out?"

"You put me out!" ses Sam, who 'ad tied 'is clothes up with string while 'e was in the stable, and 'ad got his arms free.

The cabman looked at 'im 'elpless for a moment, and then he got up and drove off agin. At fust Sam thought 'e was going to drive back to the stable, and he clinched 'is teeth and made up 'is mind to 'ave a fight for it. Then he saw that 'e was really being driven 'ome, and at last the cab pulled up in the next street to 'is lodgings, and the cabman, asking a man to give an eye to his 'orse, walked on with the letter. He was back agin in a few minutes, and Sam could see by 'is face that something had 'appened.

"They ain't been 'ome all night," he ses, sulky-like.

"Well, I shall 'ave to send the money on to you," ses Sam, in a off-hand way. "Unless you like to call for it."

"I'll call for it, matey," ses the cabman, with a kind smile, as he took 'old of his 'orse and led it up to Sam's lodgings. "I know I can trust you, but it'll save you trouble. But s'pose he's been on the drink and lost the money?"

Sam got out and made a dash for the door, which 'appened to be open. "It won't make no difference," he ses.

"No difference?" ses the cabman, staring.

"Not to you, I mean," ses Sam, shutting the door very slow. "So long."

A DISCIPLINARIAN

There's no doubt about it," said the night watchman, "but what dissipline's a very good thing, but it don't always act well. For instance, I ain't allowed to smoke on this wharf, so when I want a pipe I either 'ave to go over to the 'Queen's 'ed,' or sit in a lighter. If I'm in the 'Queen's 'ed' I can't look arter the wharf, an' once when I was sitting in a lighter smoking the chap come aboard an' cast off afore I knew what he was doing, an' took me all the way to Greenwich. He said he'd often played that trick on watchmen.

"The worst man for dissipline I ever shipped with was Cap'n Tasker, of the Lapwing. He'd got it on the brain bad. He was a prim, clean-shaved man except for a little side-whisker, an' always used to try an' look as much like a naval officer as possible.

"I never 'ad no sort of idea what he was like when I jined the ship, an' he was quite quiet and peaceable until we was out in the open water. Then the cloven hoof showed itself, an' he kicked one o' the men for coming on deck with a dirty face, an' though the man told him he never did wash becos his skin was so delikit, he sent the bos'en to turn the hose on him.

"The bos'en seemed to take a hand in everything. We used to do everything by his whistle, it was never out of his mouth scarcely, and I've known that man to dream of it o' nights, and sit up in his sleep an' try an' blow his thumb. He whistled us to swab decks, whistled us to grub, whistled us to every blessed thing.

"Though we didn't belong to any reg'ler line, we'd got a lot o' passengers aboard, going to the Cape, an' they thought a deal o' the skipper. There was one young leftenant aboard who said he reminded him o' Nelson, an' him an' the skipper was as thick as two thieves. Nice larky young chap he was, an' more than one o' the crew tried to drop things on him from aloft when he wasn't looking.

"Every morning at ten we was inspected by the skipper, but that wasn't enough for the leftenant, and he persuaded the old man to drill us. He said it would do us good an' amuse the passengers, an' we 'ad to do all sorts of silly things with our arms an' legs, an' twice he walked the skipper to the other end of the ship, leaving twenty-three sailor-men bending over touching their toes, an' wondering whether they'd ever stand straight again.

"The very worst thing o' the lot was the boat-drill. A chap might be sitting comfortable at his grub, or having a pipe in his bunk, when the bos'en's whistle would scream out to him that the ship was sinking, an' the passengers drownding, and he was to come an' git the boats out an' save 'em. Nice sort o' game it was too. We had to run like mad with kegs o' water an' bags o' biscuit, an' then run the boats out an' launch 'em. All the men were told off to certain boats, an' the passengers too. The only difference was, if a passenger didn't care about taking a hand in the game he didn't, but we had to.

"One o' the passengers who didn't play was Major Miggens. He was very much agin it, an' called it tomfoolery; he never would go to his boat, but used to sit and sneer all the time.

"'It's only teaching the men to cut an' run,' he said to the skipper one day; 'if there ever was any need they'd run to the boats an' leave us here. Don't tell me.'

"'That's not the way I should ha' expected to hear you speak of British sailors, major,' ses the skipper rather huffy.

"'British swearers,' ses the major, sniffing. 'You don't hear their remarks when that whistle is blown. It's enough to bring a judgment on the ship.'

"'If you can point 'em out to me I'll punish 'em,' says the skipper very warm.

"'I'm not going to point 'em out,' ses the major. 'I symperthise with 'em too much. They don't get any of their beauty sleep, pore chaps, an' they want it, every one of 'em.'

"I thought that was a very kind remark o' the major to make, but o' course some of the wimmin larfed. I s'pose they think men don't want beauty sleep, as it's called.

"I heard the leftenant symperthising with the skipper arter that. He said the major was simply jealous because the men drilled so beautifully, an' then they walked aft, the leftenant talking very earnest an' the skipper shaking his head at something he was saying.

"It was just two nights arter this. I'd gone below an' turned in when I began to dream that the major had borrowed the bos'en's whistle an' was practising on it. I remember thinking in my sleep what a comfort it was it was only the major, when one of the chaps give me a dig in the back an' woke me.

"'Tumble up,' ses he, 'the ship's afire.'

"I rushed up on deck, an' there was no mistake about who was blowing the whistle. The bell was jangling horrible, smoke was rolling up from the hatches, an' some o' the men was dragging out the hose an' tripping up the passengers with it as they came running up on deck. The noise and confusion was fearful.

"'Out with the boats,' ses Tom Hall to me, 'don't you hear the whistle?'

"'What, ain't we going to try an' put the fire out?' I ses.

"'Obey orders,' ses Tom, 'that's what we've got to do, an' the sooner we're away the better. You know what's in her.'

"We ran to the boats then, an', I must say, we got 'em out well, and the very fust person to git into mine was the major in his piejammers; arter all the others was in we 'ad 'im out agin. He didn't belong to our boat, an' dissipline is dissipline any day.

"Afore we could git clear o' the ship, however, he came yelling to the side an' said his boat had gone, an' though we prodded him with our oars he lowered himself over the side and dropped in.

"Fortunately for us it was a lovely clear night; there was no moon, but the stars were very bright. The engines had stopped, an' the old ship sat on the water scarcely moving. Another boat was bumping up against ours, and two more came creeping round the bows from the port side an' jined us.

"'Who's in command?' calls out the major.

"'I am,' ses the first mate very sharp-like from one of the boats.

"'Where's the cap'n then?' called out an old lady from my boat, 'o' the name o' Prendergast.'

"'He's standing by the ship,' ses the mate.

"'Doing what?' ses Mrs. Prendergast, looking at the water as though she expected to see the skipper standing there.

"'He's going down with the ship,' ses one o' the chaps.

"Then Mrs. Prendergast asked somebody to be kind enough to lend her a handkerchief, becos she had left her pocket behind aboard ship, and began to sob very bitter.

"'Just a simple British sailor,' ses she, snivelling, 'going down with his ship. There he is. Look! On the bridge.'

"We all looked, an' then some o' the other wimmin wanted to borrer handkerchiefs. I lent one of 'em a little cotton waste, but she was so unpleasant about its being a trifle oily that she forgot all about crying, and said she'd tell the mate about me as soon as ever we got ashore.

"'I'll remember him in my prayers,' ses one o' the wimmin who was crying comfortable in a big red bandana belonging to one o' the men.

"'All England shall ring with his deed,' ses another.

"'Sympathy's cheap,' ses one of the men passengers solemnly. 'If we ever reach land we must all band together to keep his widow an' orphans.'

"'Hear, hear,' cries everybody.

"'And we'll put up a granite tombstone to his memory,' ses Mrs. Prendergast.

"'S'pose we pull back to the ship an' take him off,' ses a gentleman from another boat. 'I'm thinking it 'ud come cheaper, an' perhaps the puir mon would really like it better himself.'

"'Shame,' ses most of 'em; an' I reely b'leeve they'd worked theirselves up to that pitch they'd ha' felt disapponted if the skipper had been saved.

"We pulled along slowly, the mate's boat leading, looking back every now and then at the old ship, and wondering when she would go off, for she'd got that sort o' stuff in her hold which 'ud send her up with a bang as soon as the fire got to it; an' we was all waiting for the shock.

"'Do you know where we're going, Mr. Bunce?' calls out the major.

"'Yes,' ses the mate.

"'What's the nearest land?' asks the major.

"'Bout a thousand miles,' ses the mate.

"Then the major went into figgers, an' worked out that it 'ud take us about ten days to reach land and three to reach the bottom o' the water kegs. He shouted that out to the mate; an' the young leftenant what was in the mate's boat smoking a big cigar said there'd be quite a run on granite tombstones. He said it was a blessed thing he had disinherited his children for marrying agin his wishes, so there wouldn't be any orphans left to mourn for him.

"Some o' the wimmin smiled a little at this, an' old Mrs. Prendergast shook so that she made the boat rock. We got quite cheerful somehow, and one of the other men spoke up and said that owing to his only having reckoned two pints to the gallon, the major's figgers wasn't to be relied upon.

"We got more cheerful then, and we was beginning to look on it as just a picnic, when I'm blest if the mate's boat didn't put about and head for the ship agin.

"There was a commotion then if you like, everybody talking and laughing at once; and Mrs. Prendergast said that such a thing as one single-handed cap'n staying behind to go down with his ship, and then putting the fire out all by himself after his men had fled, had never been heard of before, an' she believed it never would be again. She said he must be terribly burnt, and he'd have to be put to bed and wrapped up in oily rags.

"It didn't take us long to get aboard agin, and the ladies fairly mobbed the skipper. Tom Hall swore as 'ow Mrs. Prendergast tried to kiss him, an' the fuss they made of him was ridiculous. I heard the clang of the telegraph in the engine-room soon as the boats was hoisted up, the engines started, and off we went again.

"'Speech,' yells out somebody. 'Speech.'

"'Bravo!' ses the others. 'Bravo!"

"Then the skipper stood up an' made 'em a nice little speech. First of all he thanked 'em for their partiality and kindness shown to him, and the orderly way in which they had left the ship. He said it reflected credit on all concerned, crew and passengers, an' no doubt they'd be surprised when he told them that there hadn't been any fire at all, but that it was just a test to make sure that the boat drill was properly understood.

"He was quite right about them being surprised. Noisy, too, they was, an' the things they said about the man they'd just been wanting to give granite tombstones to was simply astonishing. It would have taken a whole cemetery o' tombstones to put down all they said about him, and then they'd ha' had to cut the letters small.

"I vote we have an indignation meeting in the saloon to record our disgust at the cap'n's behaviour,' ses the major fiercely. 'I beg to propose that Mr. Macpherson take the chair.'

"'I second that,' ses another, fierce-like.

"'I beg to propose the major instead,' ses somebody else in a heasy off-hand sort o' way; 'Mr. Macpherson's boat not having come back yet.'

"At first everybody thought he was joking, but when they found he was really speaking the truth the excitement was awful. Fortunately, as Mrs. Prendergast remarked, there was no ladies in the boat, but there was several men passengers. We were doing a good thirteen knots an hour, but we brought up at once, an' then we 'ad the most lovely firework display I ever see aboard ship in my life. Blue lights and rockets and guns going all night, while we cruised slowly about, and the passengers sat on deck arguing as to whether the skipper would be hung or only imprisoned for life.

"It was daybreak afore we sighted them, just a little speck near the sky-line, an' we bore down on them for all we was worth. Half an hour later they was alongside, an' of all the chilly, miserable-looking men I ever see they was the worst.

"They had to be helped up the side a'most, and they was so grateful it was quite affecting, until the true state o' things was explained to them. It seemed to change 'em wonderful, an' after Mr. Macpherson had had three cups o' hot coffee an' four glasses o' brandy he took the chair at the indignation meeting, an' went straight off to sleep in it. They woke him up three times, but he was so cross about it that the ladies had to go away an' the meeting was adjourned.

"I don't think it ever came to much after all, nobody being really hurt, an' the skipper being so much upset they felt sort o' sorry for 'im.

"The rest of the passage was very quiet an' comfortable, but o' course it all came out at the other end, an' the mate brought the ship home. Some o' the chaps said the skipper was a bit wrong in the 'ed, and, while I'm not gainsaying that, it's my firm opinion that he was persuaded to do what he did by that young leftenant. As I said afore, he was a larky young chap, an' very fond of a joke if he didn't have to pay for it."

A DISTANT RELATIVE

Mr. Potter had just taken Ethel Spriggs into the kitchen to say good-by; in the small front room Mr. Spriggs, with his fingers already fumbling at the linen collar of ceremony, waited impatiently.

"They get longer and longer over their good-bys," he complained.

"It's only natural," said Mrs. Spriggs, looking up from a piece of fine sewing. "Don't you remember—"

"No, I don't," said her husband, doggedly. "I know that your pore father never 'ad to put on a collar for me; and, mind you, I won't wear one after they're married, not if you all went on your bended knees and asked me to."

He composed his face as the door opened, and nodded good-night to the rather over-dressed young man who came through the room with his daughter.

The latter opened the front-door and passing out with Mr. Potter, held it slightly open. A penetrating draught played upon the exasperated Mr. Spriggs. He coughed loudly.

"Your father's got a cold," said Mr. Potter, in a concerned voice.

"No; it's only too much smoking," said the girl. "He's smoking all day long."

The indignant Mr. Spriggs coughed again; but the young people had found a new subject of conversation. It ended some minutes later in a playful scuffle, during which the door acted the part of a ventilating fan.

"It's only for another fortnight," said Mrs. Spriggs, hastily, as her husband rose.

"After they're spliced," said the vindictive Mr. Spriggs, resuming his seat, "I'll go round and I'll play about with their front-door till—"

He broke off abruptly as his daughter, darting into the room, closed the door with a bang that nearly extinguished the lamp, and turned the key. Before her flushed and laughing face Mr. Spriggs held his peace.

"What's the matter?" she asked, eying him. "What are you looking like that for?"

"Too much draught—for your mother," said Mr. Spriggs, feebly. "I'm afraid of her asthma agin."

He fell to work on the collar once more, and, escaping at last from the clutches of that enemy, laid it on the table and unlaced his boots. An attempt to remove his coat was promptly frustrated by his daughter.

"You'll get doing it when you come round to see us," she explained.

Mr. Spriggs sighed, and lighting a short clay pipe—forbidden in the presence of his future son-in-law—fell to watching mother and daughter as they gloated over dress materials and discussed double-widths.

"Anybody who can't be 'appy with her," he said, half an hour later, as his daughter slapped his head by way of bidding him good-night, and retired, "don't deserve to be 'appy."

"I wish it was over," whispered his wife. "She'll break her heart if anything happens, and—and Gussie will be out now in a day or two."

"A gal can't 'elp what her uncle does," said Mr. Spriggs, fiercely; "if Alfred throws her over for that, he's no man."

"Pride is his great fault," said his wife, mournfully.

"It's no good taking up troubles afore they come," observed Mr. Spriggs. "P'r'aps Gussie won't come 'ere."

"He'll come straight here," said his wife, with conviction; "he'll come straight here and try and make a fuss of me, same as he used to do when we was children and I'd got a ha'penny. I know him."

"Cheer up, old gal," said Mr. Spriggs; "if he does, we must try and get rid of 'im; and, if he won't go, we must tell Alfred that he's been to Australia, same as we did Ethel."

His wife smiled faintly.

"That's the ticket," continued Mr. Spriggs. "For one thing, I b'leeve he'll be ashamed to show his face here; but, if he does, he's come back from Australia. See? It'll make it nicer for 'im too. You don't suppose he wants to boast of where he's been?"

"And suppose he comes while Alfred is here?" said his wife.

"Then I say, 'How 'ave you left 'em all in Australia?' and wink at him," said the ready Mr. Spriggs.

"And s'pose you're not here?" objected his wife.

"Then you say it and wink at him," was the reply. "No; I know you can't," he added, hastily, as Mrs. Spriggs raised another objection; "you've been too well brought up. Still, you can try."

It was a slight comfort to Mrs. Spriggs that Mr. Augustus Price did, after all, choose a convenient time for his reappearance. A faint knock sounded on the door two days afterwards as she sat at tea with her husband, and an anxious face with somewhat furtive eyes was thrust into the room.

"Emma!" said a mournful voice, as the upper part of the intruder's body followed the face.

"Gussie!" said Mrs. Spriggs, rising in disorder.

Mr. Price drew his legs into the room, and, closing the door with extraordinary care, passed the cuff of his coat across his eyes and surveyed them tenderly.

"I've come home to die," he said, slowly, and, tottering across the room, embraced his sister with much unction.

"What are you going to die of?" inquired Mr. Spriggs, reluctantly accepting the extended hand.

"Broken 'art, George," replied his brother-in-law, sinking into a chair.

Mr. Spriggs grunted, and, moving his chair a little farther away, watched the intruder as his wife handed him a plate. A troubled glance from his wife reminded him of their arrangements for the occasion, and he cleared his throat several times in vain attempts to begin.

"I'm sorry that we can't ask you to stay with us, Gussie, 'specially as you're so ill," he said, at last; "but p'r'aps you'll be better after picking a bit."

Mr. Price, who was about to take a slice of bread and butter, refrained, and, closing his eyes, uttered a faint moan. "I sha'n't last the night," he muttered.

"That's just it," said Mr. Spriggs, eagerly. "You see, Ethel is going to be married in a fortnight, and if you died here that would put it off."

"I might last longer if I was took care of," said the other, opening his eyes.

"And, besides, Ethel don't know where you've been," continued Mr. Spriggs. "We told 'er that you had gone to Australia. She's going to marry a very partikler young chap—a grocer—and if he found it out it might be awk'ard."

Mr. Price closed his eyes again, but the lids quivered.

"It took 'im some time to get over me being a bricklayer," pursued Mr. Spriggs. "What he'd say to you—"

"Tell 'im I've come back from Australia, if you like," said Mr. Price, faintly. "I don't mind."

Mr. Spriggs cleared his throat again. "But, you see, we told Ethel as you was doing well out there," he said, with an embarrassed laugh, "and girl-like, and Alfred talking a good deal about his relations, she— she's made the most of it."

"It don't matter," said the complaisant Mr. Price; "you say what you like. I sha'n't interfere with you."

"But, you see, you don't look as though you've been making money," said his sister, impatiently. "Look at your clothes."

Mr. Price held up his hand. "That's easy got over," he remarked; "while I'm having a bit of tea George can go out and buy me some new ones. You get what you think I should look richest in, George—a black tail-coat would be best, I should think, but I leave it to you. A bit of a fancy waistcoat, p'r'aps, lightish trousers, and a pair o' nice boots, easy sevens."

He sat upright in his chair and, ignoring the look of consternation that passed between husband and wife, poured himself out a cup of tea and took a slice of cake.

"Have you got any money?" said Mr. Spriggs, after a long pause.

"I left it behind me—in Australia," said Mr. Price, with ill-timed facetiousness.

"Getting better, ain't you?" said his brother-in-law, sharply. "How's that broken 'art getting on?"

"It'll go all right under a fancy waistcoat," was the reply; "and while you're about it, George, you'd better get me a scarf-pin, and, if you could run to a gold watch and chain—"

He was interrupted by a frenzied outburst from Mr. Spriggs; a somewhat incoherent summary of Mr. Price's past, coupled with unlawful and heathenish hopes for his future.

"You're wasting time," said Mr. Price, calmly, as he paused for breath. "Don't get 'em if you don't want to. I'm trying to help you, that's all. I don't mind anybody knowing where I've been. I was innercent. If you will give way to sinful pride you must pay for it."

Mr. Spriggs, by a great effort, regained his self-control. "Will you go away if I give you a quid?" he asked, quietly.

"No," said Mr. Price, with a placid smile. "I've got a better idea of the value of money than that. Besides, I want to see my dear niece, and see whether that young man's good enough for her."

"Two quid?" suggested his brother-in-law.

Mr. Price shook his head. "I couldn't do it," he said, calmly. "In justice to myself I couldn't do it. You'll be feeling lonely when you lose Ethel, and I'll stay and keep you company."

The bricklayer nearly broke out again; but, obeying a glance from his wife, closed his lips and followed her obediently upstairs. Mr. Price, filling his pipe from a paper of tobacco on the mantelpiece, winked at himself encouragingly in the glass, and smiled gently as he heard the chinking of coins upstairs.

"Be careful about the size," he said, as Mr. Spriggs came down and took his hat from a nail; "about a couple of inches shorter than yourself and not near so much round the waist."

Mr. Spriggs regarded him sternly for a few seconds, and then, closing the door with a bang, went off down the street. Left alone, Mr. Price strolled about the room investigating, and then, drawing an easy-chair up to the fire, put his feet on the fender and relapsed into thought.

Two hours later he sat in the same place, a changed and resplendent being. His thin legs were hidden in light check trousers, and the companion waistcoat to Joseph's Coat graced the upper part of his body. A large chrysanthemum in the button-hole of his frock-coat completed the picture of an Australian millionaire, as understood by Mr. Spriggs.

"A nice watch and chain, and a little money in my pockets, and I shall be all right," murmured Mr. Price.

"You won't get any more out o' me," said Mr. Spriggs, fiercely. "I've spent every farthing I've got."

"Except what's in the bank," said his brother-in-law. "It'll take you a day or two to get at it, I know. S'pose we say Saturday for the watch and chain?"

Mr. Spriggs looked helplessly at his wife, but she avoided his gaze. He turned and gazed in a fascinated fashion at Mr. Price, and received a cheerful nod in return.

"I'll come with you and help choose it," said the latter. "It'll save you trouble if it don't save your pocket."

He thrust his hands in his trouser-pockets and, spreading his legs wide apart, tilted his head back and blew smoke to the ceiling. He was in the same easy position when Ethel arrived home accompanied by Mr. Potter.

"It's—it's your Uncle Gussie," said Mrs. Spriggs, as the girl stood eying the visitor.

"From Australia," said her husband, thickly.

Mr. Price smiled, and his niece, noticing that he removed his pipe and wiped his lips with the back of his hand, crossed over and kissed his eyebrow. Mr. Potter was then introduced and received a gracious reception, Mr. Price commenting on the extraordinary likeness he bore to a young friend of his who had just come in for forty thousand a year.

"That's nearly as much as you're worth, uncle, isn't it?" inquired Miss Spriggs, daringly.

Mr. Price shook his head at her and pondered. "Rather more," he said, at last, "rather more."

Mr. Potter caught his breath sharply; Mr. Spriggs, who was stooping to get a light for his pipe, nearly fell into the fire. There was an impressive silence.

"Money isn't everything," said Mr. Price, looking round and shaking his head. "It's not much good, except to give away."

His eye roved round the room and came to rest finally upon Mr. Potter. The young man noticed with a thrill that it beamed with benevolence.

"Fancy coming over without saying a word to anybody, and taking us all by surprise like this!" said Ethel.

"I felt I must see you all once more before I died," said her uncle, simply. "Just a flying visit I meant it to be, but your father and mother won't hear of my going back just yet."

"Of course not," said Ethel, who was helping the silent Mrs. Spriggs to lay supper.

"When I talked of going your father 'eld me down in my chair," continued the veracious Mr. Price.

"Quite right, too," said the girl. "Now draw your chair up and have some supper, and tell us all about Australia."

Mr. Price drew his chair up, but, as to talking about Australia, he said ungratefully that he was sick of the name of the place, and preferred instead to discuss the past and future of Mr. Potter. He learned, among other things, that that gentleman was of a careful and thrifty disposition, and that his savings, augmented by a lucky legacy, amounted to a hundred and ten pounds.

"Alfred is going to stay with Palmer and Mays for another year, and then we shall take a business of our own," said Ethel.

"Quite right," said Mr. Price. "I like to see young people make their own way," he added meaningly. "It's good for 'em."

It was plain to all that he had taken a great fancy to Mr. Potter. He discussed the grocery trade with the air of a rich man seeking a good investment, and threw out dark hints about returning to England after a final visit to Australia and settling down in the bosom of his family. He accepted a cigar from Mr. Potter after supper, and, when the young man left—at an unusually late hour—walked home with him.

It was the first of several pleasant evenings, and Mr. Price, who had bought a book dealing with Australia from a second-hand bookstall, no longer denied them an account of his adventures there. A gold watch and chain, which had made a serious hole in his brother-in-law's Savings Bank account, lent an air of substance to his waistcoat, and a pin of excellent paste sparkled in his neck-tie. Under the influence of good food and home comforts he improved every day, and the unfortunate Mr. Spriggs was at his wits' end to resist further encroachments. From the second day of their acquaintance he called Mr. Potter "Alf," and the young people listened with great attention to his discourse on "Money: How to Make It and How to Keep It."

His own dealings with Mr. Spriggs afforded an example which he did not quote. Beginning with shillings, he led up to half-crowns, and, encouraged by success, one afternoon boldly demanded a half-sovereign to buy a wedding-present with. Mrs. Spriggs drew her over-wrought husband into the kitchen and argued with him in whispers.

"Give him what he wants till they're married," she entreated; "after that Alfred can't help himself, and it'll be as much to his interest to keep quiet as anybody else."

Mr. Spriggs, who had been a careful man all his life, found the half-sovereign and a few new names, which he bestowed upon Mr. Price at the same time. The latter listened unmoved. In fact, a bright eye and a pleasant smile seemed to indicate that he regarded them rather in the nature of compliments than otherwise.

"I telegraphed over to Australia this morning," he said, as they all sat at supper that evening.

"About my money?" said Mr. Potter, eagerly.

Mr. Price frowned at him swiftly. "No; telling my head clerk to send over a wedding-present for you," he said, his face softening under the eye of Mr. Spriggs. "I've got just the thing for you there. I can't see anything good enough over here."

The young couple were warm in their thanks.

"What did you mean, about your money?" inquired Mr. Spriggs, turning to his future son-in-law.

"Nothing," said the young man, evasively.

"It's a secret," said Mr. Price.

"What about?" persisted Mr. Spriggs, raising his voice.

"It's a little private business between me and Uncle Gussie," said Mr. Potter, somewhat stiffly.

"You—you haven't been lending him money?" stammered the bricklayer.

"Don't be silly, father," said Miss Spriggs, sharply. "What good would Alfred's little bit o' money be to Uncle Gussie? If you must know, Alfred is drawing it out for uncle to invest it for him."

The eyes of Mr. and Mrs. Spriggs and Mr. Price engaged in a triangular duel. The latter spoke first.

"I'm putting it into my business for him," he said, with a threatening glance, "in Australia."

"And he didn't want his generosity known," added Mr. Potter.

The bewildered Mr. Spriggs looked helplessly round the table. His wife's foot pressed his, and like a mechanical toy his lips snapped together.

"I didn't know you had got your money handy," said Mrs. Spriggs, in trembling tones.

"I made special application, and I'm to have it on Friday," said Mr. Potter, with a smile. "You don't get a chance like that every day."

He filled Uncle Gussie's glass for him, and that gentleman at once raised it and proposed the health of the young couple. "If anything was to 'appen to break it off now," he said, with a swift glance at his sister, "they'd be miserable for life, I can see that."

"Miserable for ever," assented Mr. Potter, in a sepulchral voice, as he squeezed the hand of Miss Spriggs under the table.

"It's the only thing worth 'aving—love," continued Mr. Price, watching his brother-in-law out of the corner of his eye. "Money is nothing."

Mr. Spriggs emptied his glass and, knitting his brows, drew patterns on the cloth with the back of his knife. His wife's foot was still pressing on his, and he waited for instructions.

For once, however, Mrs. Spriggs had none to give. Even when Mr. Potter had gone and Ethel had retired upstairs she was still voiceless. She sat for some time looking at the fire and stealing an occasional glance at Uncle Gussie as he smoked a cigar; then she arose and bent over her husband.

"Do what you think best," she said, in a weary voice. "Good-night."

"What about that money of young Alfred's?" demanded Mr. Spriggs, as the door closed behind her.

"I'm going to put it in my business," said Uncle Gussie, blandly; "my business in Australia."

"Ho! You've got to talk to me about that first," said the other.

His brother-in-law leaned back and smoked with placid enjoyment. "You do what you like," he said, easily. "Of course, if you tell Alfred, I sha'n't get the money, and Ethel won't get 'im. Besides that, he'll find out what lies you've been telling."

"I wonder you can look me in the face," said the raging bricklayer.

"And I should give him to understand that you were going shares in the hundred and ten pounds and then thought better of it," said the unmoved Mr. Price. "He's the sort o' young chap as'll believe anything. Bless 'im!"

Mr. Spriggs bounced up from his chair and stood over him with his fists clinched. Mr. Price glared defiance.

"If you're so partikler you can make it up to him," he said, slowly. "You've been a saving man, I know, and Emma 'ad a bit left her that I ought to have 'ad. When you've done play-acting I'll go to bed. So long!"

He got up, yawning, and walked to the door, and Mr. Spriggs, after a momentary idea of breaking him in pieces and throwing him out into the street, blew out the lamp and went upstairs to discuss the matter with his wife until morning.

Mr. Spriggs left for his work next day with the question still undecided, but a pretty strong conviction that Mr. Price would have to have his way. The wedding was only five days off, and the house was in a bustle of preparation. A certain gloom which he could not shake off he attributed to a raging toothache, turning a deaf ear to the various remedies suggested by Uncle Gussie, and the name of an excellent dentist who had broken a tooth of Mr. Potter's three times before extracting it.

Uncle Gussie he treated with bare civility in public, and to blood-curdling threats in private. Mr. Price, ascribing the latter to the toothache, also varied his treatment to his company; prescribing whisky held in the mouth, and other agreeable remedies when there were listeners, and recommending him to fill his mouth with cold water and sit on the fire till it boiled, when they were alone.

He was at his worst on Thursday morning; on Thursday afternoon he came home a bright and contented man. He hung his cap on the nail with a flourish, kissed his wife, and, in full view of the disapproving Mr. Price, executed a few clumsy steps on the hearthrug.

"Come in for a fortune?" inquired the latter, eying him sourly.

"No; I've saved one," replied Mr. Spriggs, gayly. "I wonder I didn't think of it myself."

"Think of what?" inquired Mr. Price.

"You'll soon know," said Mr. Spriggs, "and you've only got yourself to thank for it."

Uncle Gussie sniffed suspiciously; Mrs. Spriggs pressed for particulars.

"I've got out of the difficulty," said her husband, drawing his chair to the tea-table. "Nobody'll suffer but Gussie."

"Ho!" said that gentleman, sharply.

"I took the day off," said Mr. Spriggs, smiling contentedly at his wife, "and went to see a friend of mine, Bill White the policeman, and told him about Gussie."

Mr. Price stiffened in his chair.

"Acting—under—his—advice," said Mr. Spriggs, sipping his tea, "I wrote to Scotland Yard and told 'em that Augustus Price, ticket-of-leave man, was trying to obtain a hundred and ten pounds by false pretences."

Mr. Price, white and breathless, rose and confronted him.

"The beauty o' that is, as Bill says," continued Mr. Spriggs, with much enjoyment, "that Gussie'll 'ave to set out on his travels again. He'll have to go into hiding, because if they catch him he'll 'ave to finish his time. And Bill says if he writes letters to any of us it'll only make it easier to find him. You'd better take the first train to Australia, Gussie."

"What—what time did you post—the letter?" inquired Uncle Gussie, jerkily.

"'Bout two o'clock," said Mr. Spriggs, glaring at the clock. "I reckon you've just got time."

Mr. Price stepped swiftly to the small sideboard, and, taking up his hat, clapped it on. He paused a moment at the door to glance up and down the street, and then the door closed softly behind him. Mrs. Spriggs looked at her husband.

"Called away to Australia by special telegram," said the latter, winking. "Bill White is a trump; that's what he is."

"Oh, George!" said his wife. "Did you really write that letter?"

Mr. Spriggs winked again.

A GARDEN PLOT

The able-bodied men of the village were at work, the children were at school singing the multiplication-table lullaby, while the wives and mothers at home nursed the baby with one hand and did the housework with the other. At the end of the village an old man past work sat at a rough deal table under the creaking signboard of the Cauliflower, gratefully drinking from a mug of ale supplied by a chance traveller who sat opposite him.

The shade of the elms was pleasant and the ale good. The traveller filled his pipe and, glancing at the dusty hedges and the white road baking in the sun, called for the mugs to be refilled, and pushed his pouch towards his companion. After which he paid a compliment to the appearance of the village.

"It ain't what it was when I was a boy," quavered the old man, filling his pipe with trembling fingers. "I mind when the grindstone was stuck just outside the winder o' the forge instead o' being one side as it now is; and as for the shop winder—it's twice the size it was when I was a young 'un."

He lit his pipe with the scientific accuracy of a smoker of sixty years' standing, and shook his head solemnly as he regarded his altered birthplace. Then his colour heightened and his dim eye flashed.

"It's the people about 'ere 'as changed more than the place 'as," he said, with sudden fierceness; "there's a set o' men about here nowadays as are no good to anybody; reg'lar raskels. And if you've the mind to listen I can tell you of one or two as couldn't be beat in London itself.

"There's Tom Adams for one. He went and started wot 'e called a Benevolent Club. Threepence a week each we paid agin sickness or accident, and Tom was secretary. Three weeks arter the club was started he caught a chill and was laid up for a month. He got back to work a week, and then 'e sprained something in 'is leg; and arter that was well 'is inside went wrong. We didn't think much of it at first, not understanding figures; but at the end o' six months the club hadn't got a farthing, and they was in Tom's debt one pound seventeen-and-six.

"He isn't the only one o' that sort in the place, either. There was Herbert Richardson. He went to town, and came back with the idea of a Goose Club for Christmas. We paid twopence a week into that for pretty near ten months, and then Herbert went back to town agin, and all we 'ear of 'im, through his sister, is that he's still there and doing well, and don't know when he'll be back.

"But the artfullest and worst man in this place—and that's saying a good deal, mind you—is Bob Pretty. Deep is no word for 'im. There's no way of being up to 'im. It's through 'im that we lost our Flower Show; and, if you'd like to 'ear the rights o' that, I don't suppose there's anybody in this place as knows as much about it as I do—barring Bob hisself that is, but 'e wouldn't tell it to you as plain as I can.

"We'd only 'ad the Flower Show one year, and little anybody thought that the next one was to be the last. The first year you might smell the place a mile off in the summer, and on the day of the show people came from a long way round, and brought money to spend at the Cauliflower and other places.

"It was started just after we got our new parson, and Mrs. Pawlett, the parson's wife, 'is name being Pawlett, thought as she'd encourage men to love their 'omes and be better 'usbands by giving a prize every year for the best cottage garden. Three pounds was the prize, and a metal tea-pot with writing on it.

"As I said, we only 'ad it two years. The fust year the garden as got it was a picter, and Bill Chambers, 'im as won the prize, used to say as 'e was out o' pocket by it, taking 'is time and the money 'e spent on flowers. Not as we believed that, you understand, 'specially as Bill did 'is very best to get it the next year, too. 'E didn't get it, and though p'r'aps most of us was glad 'e didn't, we was all very surprised at the way it turned out in the end.

"The Flower Show was to be 'eld on the 5th o' July, just as a'most everything about here was at its best. On the 15th of June Bill Chambers's garden seemed to be leading, but Peter Smith and Joe Gubbins and Sam Jones and Henery Walker was almost as good, and it was understood that more than one of 'em had got a surprise which they'd produce at the last moment, too late for the others to copy. We used to sit up here of an evening at this Cauliflower public-house and put money on it. I put mine on Henery Walker, and the time I spent in 'is garden 'elping 'im is a sin and a shame to think of.

"Of course some of 'em used to make fun of it, and Bob Pretty was the worst of 'em all. He was always a lazy, good-for-nothing man, and 'is garden was a disgrace. He'd chuck down any rubbish in it: old bones, old tins, bits of an old bucket, anything to make it untidy. He used to larf at 'em awful about their gardens and about being took up by the parson's wife. Nobody ever see 'im do any work, real 'ard work, but the smell from 'is place at dinner-time was always nice, and I believe that he knew more about game than the parson hisself did.

"It was the day arter this one I'm speaking about, the 16th o' June, that the trouble all began, and it came about in a very eggstrordinary way. George English, a quiet man getting into years, who used when 'e was younger to foller the sea, and whose only misfortin was that 'e was a brother-in-law o' Bob Pretty's, his sister marrying Bob while 'e was at sea and knowing nothing about it, 'ad a letter come from a mate of his who 'ad gone to Australia to live. He'd 'ad letters from Australia before, as we all knew from Miss Wicks at the post-office, but this one upset him altogether. He didn't seem like to know what to do about it.

"While he was wondering Bill Chambers passed. He always did pass George's 'ouse about that time in the evening, it being on 'is way 'ome, and he saw George standing at 'is gate with a letter in 'is 'and looking very puzzled.

"'Evenin', George,' ses Bill.

"'Evenin',' ses George.

"'Not bad news, I 'ope?' ses Bill, noticing 'is manner, and thinking it was strange.

"'No,' ses George. 'I've just 'ad a very eggstrordinary letter from Australia,' he ses, 'that's all.'

"Bill Chambers was always a very inquisitive sort o' man, and he stayed and talked to George until George, arter fust making him swear oaths that 'e wouldn't tell a soul, took 'im inside and showed 'im the letter.

"It was more like a story-book than a letter. George's mate, John Biggs by name, wrote to say that an uncle of his who had just died, on 'is deathbed told him that thirty years ago he 'ad been in this very village, staying at this 'ere very Cauliflower, whose beer we're drinking now. In the night, when everybody was asleep, he got up and went quiet-like and buried a bag of five hundred and seventeen sovereigns and one half-sovereign in one of the cottage gardens till 'e could come for it agin. He didn't say 'ow he come by the money, and, when Bill spoke about that, George English said that, knowing the man, he was afraid 'e 'adn't come by it honest, but anyway his friend John Biggs wanted it, and, wot was more, 'ad asked 'im in the letter to get it for 'im.

"'And wot I'm to do about it, Bill,' he ses, I don't know. All the directions he gives is, that 'e thinks it was the tenth cottage on the right-'and side of the road, coming down from the Cauliflower. He thinks it's the tenth, but 'e's not quite sure. Do you think I'd better make it known and offer a reward of ten shillings, say, to any one who finds it?'

"'No,' ses Bill, shaking 'is 'ead. 'I should hold on a bit if I was you, and think it over. I shouldn't tell another single soul, if I was you.'

"'I be'leeve you're right,' ses George. 'John Biggs would never forgive me if I lost that money for 'im. You'll remember about keeping it secret, Bill?'

"Bill swore he wouldn't tell a soul, and 'e went off 'ome and 'ad his supper, and then 'e walked up the road to the Cauliflower and back, and then up and back again, thinking over what George 'ad been telling 'im, and noticing, what 'e 'd never taken the trouble to notice before, that 'is very house was the tenth one from the Cauliflower.

"Mrs. Chambers woke up at two o'clock next morning and told Bill to get up further, and then found 'e wasn't there. She was rather surprised at first, but she didn't think much of it, and thought, what happened to be true, that 'e was busy in the garden, it being a light night. She turned over and went to sleep again, and at five when she woke up she could distinctly 'ear Bill working 'is 'ardest. Then she went to the winder and nearly dropped as she saw Bill in his shirt and trousers digging away like mad. A quarter of the garden was all dug up, and she shoved open the winder and screamed out to know what 'e was doing.

"Bill stood up straight and wiped 'is face with his shirt-sleeve and started digging again, and then his wife just put something on and rushed downstairs as fast as she could go.

"'What on earth are you a-doing of, Bill?' she screams.

"'Go indoors,' ses Bill, still digging.

"'Have you gone mad?' she ses, half-crying.

"Bill just stopped to throw a lump of mould at her, and then went on digging till Henery Walker, who also thought 'e 'ad gone mad, and didn't want to stop 'im too soon, put 'is 'ead over the 'edge and asked 'im the same thing.

"'Ask no questions and you'll 'ear no lies, and keep your ugly face your own side of the 'edge,' ses Bill. 'Take it indoors and frighten the children with,' he ses. 'I don't want it staring at me.'

"Henery walked off offended, and Bill went on with his digging. He wouldn't go to work, and 'e 'ad his breakfast in the garden, and his wife spent all the morning in the front answering the neighbours' questions and begging of 'em to go in and say something to Bill. One of 'em did go, and came back a'most directly and stood there for hours telling diff'rent people wot Bill 'ad said to 'er, and asking whether 'e couldn't be locked up for it.

"By tea-time Bill was dead-beat, and that stiff he could 'ardly raise 'is bread and butter to his mouth. Several o' the chaps looked in in the evening, but all they could get out of 'im was, that it was a new way o' cultivating 'is garden 'e 'ad just 'eard of, and that those who lived the longest would see the most. By night-time 'e'd nearly finished the job, and 'is garden was just ruined.

"Afore people 'ad done talking about Bill, I'm blest if Peter Smith didn't go and cultivate 'is garden in exactly the same way. The parson and 'is wife was away on their 'oliday, and nobody could say a word. The curate who 'ad come over to take 'is place for a time, and who took the names of people for the Flower Show, did point out to 'im that he was spoiling 'is chances, but Peter was so rude to 'im that he didn't stay long enough to say much.

"When Joe Gubbins started digging up 'is garden people began to think they were all bewitched, and I went round to see Henery Walker to tell 'im wot a fine chance 'e'd got, and to remind 'im that I'd put another ninepence on 'im the night before. All 'e said was, 'More fool you,' and went on digging a 'ole in his garden big enough to put a 'ouse in.

"In a fortnight's time there wasn't a garden worth looking at in the place, and it was quite clear there'd be no Flower Show that year, and of all the silly, bad-tempered men in the place them as 'ad dug up their pretty gardens was the wust.

"It was just a few days before the day fixed for the Flower Show, and I was walking up the road when I see Joe and Henery Walker and one or two more leaning over Bob Pretty's fence and talking to 'im. I stopped, too, to see what they were looking at, and found they was watching Bob's two boys a-weeding of 'is garden. It was a disgraceful, untidy sort of place, as I said before, with a few marigolds and nasturtiums, and sich-like put in anywhere, and Bob was walking up and down smoking of 'is pipe and watching 'is wife hoe atween the plants and cut off dead marigold blooms.

"'That's a pretty garden you've got there, Bob,' ses Joe, grinning.

"'I've seen wuss,' ses Bob.

"'Going in for the Flower Show, Bob?' ses Henery, with a wink at us.

"'O' course I am,' ses Bob 'olding 'is' ead up; 'my marigolds ought to pull me through,' he ses.

"Henery wouldn't believe it at first, but when he saw Bob show 'is missus 'ow to pat the path down with the back o' the spade and hold the nails for 'er while she nailed a climbing nasturtium to the fence, he went off and fetched Bill Chambers and one or two others, and they all leaned over the fence breathing their 'ardest and a-saying of all the nasty things to Bob they could think of.

"'It's the best-kep' garden in the place,' ses Bob. 'I ain't afraid o' your new way o' cultivating flowers, Bill Chambers. Old-fashioned ways suit me best; I learnt 'ow to grow flowers from my father.'

"'You ain't 'ad the cheek to give your name in, Bob?' ses Sam Jones, staring.

"Bob didn't answer 'im. Tick those bits o' grass out o' the path, old gal,' he ses to 'is wife; 'they look untidy, and untidiness I can't abear.'

"He walked up and down smoking 'is pipe and pretending not to notice Henery Walker, wot 'ad moved farther along the fence, and was staring at some drabble-tailed-looking geraniums as if 'e'd seen 'em afore but wasn't quite sure where.

"'Admiring my geraniums, Henery?' ses Bob at last.

"'Where'd you get 'em?' ses Henery, 'ardly able to speak.

"'My florist's,' ses Bob, in a off-hand manner.

"'Your wot? asks Henery.

"'My florist,' ses Bob.

"'And who might 'e be when 'e's at home?' asked Henery.

"''Tain't so likely I'm going to tell you that,' ses Bob. 'Be reasonable, Henery, and ask yourself whether it's likely I should tell you 'is name. Why, I've never seen sich fine geraniums afore. I've been nursing 'em inside all the summer, and just planted 'em out.'

"'About two days arter I threw mine over my back fence,' ses Henery Walker, speaking very slowly.

"'Ho,' ses Bob, surprised. 'I didn't know you 'ad any geraniums, Henery. I thought you was digging for gravel this year.'

"Henery didn't answer 'im. Not because 'e didn't want to, mind you, but because he couldn't.

"'That one,' ses Bob, pointing at a broken geranium with the stem of 'is pipe, 'is a "Dook o' Wellington," and that white one there is wot I'm going to call "Pretty's Pride." That fine marigold over there, wot looks like a sunflower, is called "Golden Dreams."'

"'Come along, Henery,' ses Bill Chambers, bursting, 'come and get something to take the taste out of your mouth.'

"'I'm sorry I can't offer you a flower for your button-'ole,' ses Bob, perlitely, 'but it's getting so near the Flower Show now I can't afford it. If you chaps only knew wot pleasure was to be 'ad sitting among your innercent flowers, you wouldn't want to go to the public-house so often.'

"He shook 'is 'ead at 'em, and telling his wife to give the 'Dook o' Wellington' a mug of water, sat down in the chair agin and wiped the sweat off 'is brow.

"Bill Chambers did a bit o' thinking as they walked up the road, and by and by 'e turns to Joe Gubbins and 'e ses:

"'Seen anything o' George English lately, Joe?'

"'Yes,' ses Joe.

"'Seems to me we all 'ave,' ses Sam Jones.

"None of 'em liked to say wot was in their minds, 'aving all seen George English and swore pretty strong not to tell his secret, and none of 'em liking to own up that they'd been digging up their gardens to get money as 'e'd told 'em about. But presently Bill Chambers ses:

"'Without telling no secrets or breaking no promises, Joe, supposing a certain 'ouse was mentioned in a certain letter from forrin parts, wot 'ouse was it?'

"'Supposing it was so,' ses Joe, careful too; 'the second 'ouse counting from the Cauliflower.'

"'The ninth 'ouse, you mean,' ses Henery Walker, sharply.

"'Second 'ouse in Mill Lane, you mean,' ses Sam Jones, wot lived there.

"Then they all see 'ow they'd been done, and that they wasn't, in a manner o' speaking, referring to the same letter. They came up and sat 'ere where we're sitting now, all dazed-like. It wasn't only the chance o' losing the prize that upset 'em, but they'd wasted their time and ruined their gardens and got called mad by the other folks. Henery Walker's state o' mind was dreadful for to see, and he kep' thinking of 'orrible things to say to George English, and then being afraid they wasn't strong enough.

"While they was talking who should come along but George English hisself! He came right up to the table, and they all sat back on the bench and stared at 'im fierce, and Henery Walker crinkled 'is nose at him.

"'Evening,' he ses, but none of 'em answered im; they all looked at Henery to see wot 'e was going to say.

"'Wot's up?' ses George, in surprise.

"'Gardens,' ses Henery.

"'So I've 'eard,' ses George.

"He shook 'is 'ead and looked at them sorrowful and severe at the same time.

"'So I 'eard, and I couldn't believe my ears till I went and looked for myself,' he ses, 'and wot I want to say is this: you know wot I'm referring to. If any man 'as found wot don't belong to him 'e knows who to give it to. It ain't wot I should 'ave expected of men wot's lived in the same place as me for years. Talk about honesty,' 'e ses, shaking 'is 'ead agin, 'I should like to see a little of it.'

"Peter Smith opened his mouth to speak, and 'ardly knowing wot 'e was doing took a pull at 'is beer at the same time, and if Sam Jones 'adn't been by to thump 'im on the back I b'lieve he'd ha' died there and then.

"'Mark my words,' ses George English, speaking very slow and solemn, 'there'll be no blessing on it. Whoever's made 'is fortune by getting up and digging 'is garden over won't get no real benefit from it. He may wear a black coat and new trousers on Sunday, but 'e won't be 'appy. I'll go and get my little taste o' beer somewhere else,' 'e ses. 'I can't breathe here.'

"He walked off before any one could say a word; Bill Chambers dropped 'is pipe and smashed it, Henery Walker sat staring after 'im with 'is mouth wide open, and Sam Jones, who was always one to take advantage, drank 'is own beer under the firm belief that it was Joe's.

"'I shall take care that Mrs. Pawlett 'ears o' this,' ses Henery, at last.

"'And be asked wot you dug your garden up for,' ses Joe, 'and 'ave to explain that you broke your promise to George. Why, she'd talk at us for years and years.'

"'And parson 'ud preach a sermon about it,' ses Sam; 'where's your sense, Henery?'

"'We should be the larfing-stock for miles round,' ses Bill Chambers. 'If anybody wants to know, I dug my garden up to enrich the soil for next year, and also to give some other chap a chance of the prize.'

"Peter Smith 'as always been a unfortunit man; he's got the name for it. He was just 'aving another drink as Bill said that, and this time we all thought 'e'd gorn. He did hisself.

"Mrs. Pawlett and the parson came 'ome next day, an' 'er voice got that squeaky with surprise it was painful to listen to her. All the chaps stuck to the tale that they'd dug their garden up to give the others a chance, and Henery Walker, 'e went further and said it was owing to a sermon on unselfishness wot the curate 'ad preached three weeks afore. He 'ad a nice little red-covered 'ymn-book the next day with 'From a friend' wrote in it.

"All things considered, Mrs. Pawlett was for doing away with the Flower Show that year and giving two prizes next year instead, but one or two other chaps, encouraged by Bob's example, 'ad given in their names too, and they said it wouldn't be fair to their wives. All the gardens but one was worse than Bob's, they not having started till later than wot 'e did, and not being able to get their geraniums from 'is florist. The only better garden was Ralph Thomson's, who lived next door to 'im, but two nights afore the Flower Show 'is pig got walking in its sleep. Ralph said it was a mystery to 'im 'ow the pig could ha' got out; it must ha' put its foot through a hole too small for it, and turned the button of its door, and then climbed over a four-foot fence. He told Bob 'e wished the pig could speak, but Bob said that that was sinful and unchristian of 'im, and that most likely if it could, it would only call 'im a lot o' bad names, and ask 'im why he didn't feed it properly.

"There was quite a crowd on Flower Show day following the judges. First of all, to Bill Chambers's astonishment and surprise, they went to 'is place and stood on the 'eaps in 'is garden judging 'em, while Bill peeped at 'em through the kitchen winder 'arf-crazy. They went to every garden in the place, until one of the young ladies got tired of it, and asked Mrs. Pawlett whether they was there to judge cottage gardens or earthquakes.

"Everybody 'eld their breaths that evening in the school room when Mrs. Pawlett got up on the platform and took a slip of paper from one of the judges. She stood a moment waiting for silence, and then 'eld up her 'and to stop what she thought was clapping at the back, but which was two or three wimmen who 'ad 'ad to take their crying babies out trying to quiet 'em in the porch. Then Mrs. Pawlett put 'er glasses on her nose and just read out, short and sweet, that the prize of three sovereigns and a metal teapot for the best-kept cottage garden 'ad been won by Mr. Robert Pretty.

"One or two people patted Bob on the back as 'e walked up the middle to take the prize; then one or two more did, and Bill Chambers's pat was the 'eartiest of 'em all. Bob stopped and spoke to 'im about it.

"You would 'ardly think that Bob 'ud have the cheek to stand up there and make a speech, but 'e did. He said it gave 'im great pleasure to take the teapot and the money, and the more pleasure because 'e felt that 'e had earned 'em. He said that if 'e told 'em all 'e'd done to make sure o' the prize they'd be surprised. He said that 'e'd been like Ralph Thomson's pig, up early and late.

"He stood up there talking as though 'e was never going to leave off, and said that 'e hoped as 'is example would be of benefit to 'is neighbours. Some of 'em seemed to think that digging was everything, but 'e could say with pride that 'e 'adn't put a spade to 'is garden for three years until a week ago, and then not much.

"He finished 'is remarks by saying that 'e was going to give a tea-party up at the Cauliflower to christen the teapot, where 'e'd be pleased to welcome all friends. Quite a crowd got up and followed 'im out then, instead o' waiting for the dissolving views, and came back 'arf an hour arterwards, saying that until they'd got as far as the Cauliflower they'd no idea as Bob was so per-tikler who 'e mixed with.

"That was the last Flower Show we ever 'ad in Claybury, Mrs. Pawlett and the judges meeting the tea-party coming 'ome, and 'aving to get over a gate into a field to let it pass. What with that and Mrs. Pawlett tumbling over something further up the road, which turned out to be the teapot, smelling strong of beer, the Flower Show was given up, and the parson preached three Sundays running on the sin of beer-drinking to children who'd never 'ad any and wimmen who couldn't get it."

A GOLDEN VENTURE

The elders of the Tidger family sat at breakfast—Mrs. Tidger with knees wide apart and the youngest Tidger nestling in the valley of print-dress which lay between, and Mr. Tidger bearing on one moleskin knee a small copy of himself in a red flannel frock and a slipper. The larger Tidger children took the solids of their breakfast up and down the stone-flagged court outside, coming in occasionally to gulp draughts of very weak tea from a gallipot or two which stood on the table, and to wheedle Mr. Tidger out of any small piece of bloater which he felt generous enough to bestow.

"Peg away, Ann," said Mr. Tidger, heartily.

His wife's elder sister shook her head, and passing the remains of her slice to one of her small nephews, leaned back in her chair. "No appetite, Tidger," she said, slowly.

"You should go in for carpentering," said Mr. Tidger, in justification of the huge crust he was carving into mouthfuls with his pocket-knife. "Seems to me I can't eat enough sometimes. Hullo, who's the letter for?"

He took it from the postman, who stood at the door amid a bevy of Tidgers who had followed him up the court, and slowly read the address.

"'Mrs. Ann Pullen,'" he said, handing it over to his sister-in-law; "nice writing, too."

Mrs. Pullen broke the envelope, and after a somewhat lengthy search for her pocket, fumbled therein for her spectacles. She then searched the mantelpiece, the chest of drawers, and the dresser, and finally ran them to earth on the copper.

She was not a good scholar, and it took her some time to read the letter, a proceeding which she punctuated with such "Ohs" and "Ahs" and gaspings and "God bless my souls" as nearly drove the carpenter and his wife, who were leaning forward impatiently, to the verge of desperation.

"Who's it from?" asked Mr. Tidger for the third time.

"I don't know," said Mrs. Pullen. "Good gracious, who ever would ha' thought it!"

"Thought what, Ann?" demanded the carpenter, feverishly.

"Why don't people write their names plain?" demanded his sister-in-law, impatiently. "It's got a printed name up in the corner; perhaps that's it. Well, I never did—I don't know whether I'm standing on my head or my heels."

"You're sitting down, that's what you're a-doing," said the carpenter, regarding her somewhat unfavourably.

"Perhaps it's a take-in," said Mrs. Pullen, her lips trembling. "I've heard o' such things. If it is, I shall never get over it—never."

"Get—over—what?" asked the carpenter.

"It don't look like a take-in," soliloquized Mrs. Pullen, "and I shouldn't think anybody'd go to all that trouble and spend a penny to take in a poor thing like me."

Mr. Tidger, throwing politeness to the winds, leaped forward, and snatching the letter from her, read it with feverish haste, tempered by a defective education.

"It's a take-in, Ann," he said, his voice trembling; "it must be."

"What is?" asked Mrs. Tidger, impatiently.

"Looks like it," said Mrs. Pullen, feebly.

"What is it?" screamed Mrs. Tidger, wrought beyond all endurance.

Her husband turned and regarded her with much severity, but Mrs. Tidger's gaze was the stronger, and after a vain attempt to meet it, he handed her the letter.

Mrs. Tidger read it through hastily, and then snatching the baby from her lap, held it out with both arms to her husband, and jumping up, kissed her sister heartily, patting her on the back in her excitement until she coughed with the pain of it.

"You don't think it's a take-in, Polly?" she inquired.

"Take-in?" said her sister; "of course it ain't. Lawyers don't play jokes; their time's too valuable. No, you're an heiress all right, Ann, and I wish you joy. I couldn't be more pleased if it was myself."

She kissed her again, and going to pat her back once more, discovered that she had sunk down sufficiently low in her chair to obtain the protection of its back.

"Two thousand pounds," said Mrs. Pullen, in an awestruck voice.

"Ten hundered pounds twice over," said the carpenter, mouthing it slowly; "twenty hundered pounds."

He got up from the table, and instinctively realizing that he could not do full justice to his feelings with the baby in his arms, laid it on the teatray in a puddle of cold tea and stood looking hard at the heiress.

"I was housekeeper to her eleven years ago," said Mrs. Pullen. "I wonder what she left it to me for?"

"Didn't know what to do with it, I should think," said the carpenter, still staring openmouthed.

"Tidger, I'm ashamed of you," said his wife, snatching her infant to her bosom. "I expect you was very good to her, Ann."

"I never 'ad no luck," said the impenitent carpenter. "Nobody ever left me no money. Nobody ever left me so much as a fi-pun note."

He stared round disdainfully at his poor belongings, and drawing on his coat, took his bag from a corner, and hoisting it on his shoulder, started to his work. He scattered the news as he went, and it ran up and down the little main street of Thatcham, and thence to the outlying lanes and cottages. Within a couple of hours it was common property, and the fortunate legatee was presented with a congratulatory address every time she ventured near the door.

It is an old adage that money makes friends; the carpenter was surprised to find that the mere fact of his having a moneyed relation had the same effect, and that men to whom he had hitherto shown a certain amount of respect due to their position now sought his company. They stood him beer at the "Bell," and walked by his side through the street. When they took to dropping in of an evening to smoke a pipe the carpenter was radiant with happiness.

"You don't seem to see beyond the end of your nose, Tidger," said the wife of his bosom after they had retired one evening.

"H'm?" said the startled carpenter.

"What do you think old Miller, the dealer, comes here for?" demanded his wife.

"Smoke his pipe," replied her husband, confidently.

"And old Wiggett?" persisted Mrs. Tidger.

"Smoke his pipe," was the reply. "Why, what's the matter, Polly?"

Mrs. Tidger sniffed derisively. "You men are all alike," she snapped. "What do you think Ann wears that pink bodice for?"

"I never noticed she 'ad a pink bodice, Polly," said the carpenter.

"No? That's what I say. You men never notice anything," said his wife. "If you don't send them two old fools off, I will."

"Don't you like 'em to see Ann wearing pink?" inquired the mystified Tidger.

Mrs. Tidger bit her lip and shook her head at him scornfully. "In plain English, Tidger, as plain as I can speak it,"—she said, severely, "they're after Ann and 'er bit o' money."

Mr. Tidger gazed at her open-mouthed, and taking advantage of that fact, blew out the candle to hide his discomposure. "What!" he said, blankly, "at 'er time o' life?"

"Watch 'em to-morrer," said his wife.

The carpenter acted upon his instructions, and his ire rose as he noticed the assiduous attention paid by his two friends to the frivolous Mrs. Pullen. Mr. Wiggett, a sharp-featured little man, was doing most of the talking, while his rival, a stout, clean-shaven man with a slow, oxlike eye, looked on stolidly. Mr. Miller was seldom in a hurry, and lost many a bargain through his slowness—a fact which sometimes so painfully affected the individual who had outdistanced him that he would offer to let him have it at a still lower figure.

"You get younger than ever, Mrs. Pullen," said Wiggett, the conversation having turned upon ages.

"Young ain't the word for it," said Miller, with a praiseworthy determination not to be left behind.

"No; it's age as you're thinking of, Mr. Wiggett," said the carpenter, slowly; "none of us gets younger, do we, Ann?"

"Some of us keeps young in our ways," said Mrs. Pullen, somewhat shortly.

"How old should you say Ann is now?" persisted the watchful Tidger.

Mr. Wiggett shook his head. "I should say she's about fifteen years younger nor me," he said, slowly, "and I'm as lively as a cricket."

"She's fifty-five," said the carpenter.

"That makes you seventy, Wiggett," said Mr. Miller, pointedly. "I thought you was more than that. You look it."

Mr. Wiggett coughed sourly. "I'm fifty-nine," he growled. "Nothing 'll make me believe as Mrs.

Pullen's fifty-five, nor anywhere near it."

"Ho!" said the carpenter, on his mettle—"ho! Why, my wife here was the sixth child, and she—He caught a gleam in the sixth child's eye, and expressed her age with a cough. The others waited politely until he had finished, and Mr. Tidger, noticing this, coughed again.

"And she—" prompted Mr. Miller, displaying a polite interest.

"She ain't so young as she was," said the carpenter.

"Cares of a family," said Mr. Wiggett, plumping boldly. "I always thought Mrs. Pullen was younger than her."

"So did I," said Mr. Miller, "much younger."

Mr. Wiggett eyed him sharply. It was rather hard to have Miller hiding his lack of invention by participating in his compliments and even improving upon them. It was the way he dealt at market-listening to other dealers' accounts of their wares, and adding to them for his own.

"I was noticing you the other day, ma'am," continued Mr. Wiggett. "I see you going up the road with a step free and easy as a young girl's."

"She allus walks like that," said Mr. Miller, in a tone of surprised reproof.

"It's in the family," said the carpenter, who had been uneasily watching his wife's face.

"Both of you seem to notice a lot," said Mrs. Tidger; "much more than you used to."

Mr. Tidger, who was of a nervous and sensitive disposition, coughed again.

"You ought to take something for that cough," said Mr. Wiggett, considerately.

"Gin and beer," said Mr. Miller, with the air of a specialist.

"Bed's the best thing for it," said Mrs. Tidger, whose temper was beginning to show signs of getting out of hand.

Mr. Tidger rose and looked awkwardly at his visitors; Mr. Wiggett got up, and pretending to notice the time, said he must be going, and looked at Mr. Miller. That gentleman, who was apparently deep in some knotty problem, was gazing at the floor, and oblivious for the time to his surroundings.

"Come along," said Wiggett, with feigned heartiness, slapping him on the back.

Mr. Miller, looking for a moment as though he would like to return the compliment, came back to everyday life, and bidding the company good-night, stepped to the door, accompanied by his rival. It was immediately shut with some violence.

"They seem in a hurry," said Wiggett. "I don't think I shall go there again."

"I don't think I shall," said Mr. Miller.

After this neither of them was surprised to meet there again the next night, and indeed for several nights. The carpenter and his wife, who did not want the money to go out of the family, and were also afraid of offending Mrs. Pullen, were at their wits' end what to do. Ultimately it was resolved that Tidger, in as delicate a manner as possible, was to hint to her that they were after her money. He was so vague and so delicate that Mrs. Pullen misunderstood him, and fancying that he was trying to borrow half a crown, made him a present of five shillings.

It was evident to the slower-going Mr. Miller that his rival's tongue was giving him an advantage which only the ever-watchful presence of the carpenter and his wife prevented him from pushing to the fullest advantage. In these circumstances he sat for two hours after breakfast one morning in deep cogitation, and after six pipes got up with a twinkle in his slow eyes which his brother dealers had got to regard as a danger signal.

He had only the glimmering of an idea at first, but after a couple of pints at the "Bell" everything took shape, and he cast his eyes about for an assistant. They fell upon a man named Smith, and the dealer, after some thought, took up his glass and went over to him.

"I want you to do something for me," he remarked, in a mysterious voice.

"Ah, I've been wanting to see you," said Smith, who was also a dealer in a small way. "One o' them hins I bought off you last week is dead."

"I'll give you another for it," said Miller.

"And the others are so forgetful," continued Mr. Smith.

"Forgetful?" repeated the other.

"Forget to lay, like," said Mr. Smith, musingly.

"Never mind about them," said Mr. Miller, with some animation. "I want you to do something for me. If it comes off all right, I'll give you a dozen hins and a couple of decentish-sized pigs."

Mr. Smith called a halt. "Decentish-sized" was vague.

"Take your pick," said Mr. Miller. "You know Mrs. Pullen's got two thousand pounds—"

"Wiggett's going to have it," said the other; "he as good as told me so."

"He's after her money," said the other, sadly. "Look 'ere, Smith, I want you to tell him she's lost it all. Say that Tidger told you, but you wasn't to tell anybody else. Wiggett 'll believe you."

Mr. Smith turned upon him a face all wrinkles, lit by one eye. "I want the hins and the pigs first," he said, firmly.

Mr. Miller, shocked at his grasping spirit, stared at him mournfully.

"And twenty pounds the day you marry Mrs. Pullen," continued Mr. Smith.

Mr. Miller, leading him up and down the sawdust floor, besought him to listen to reason, and Mr. Smith allowed the better feelings of our common human nature to prevail to the extent of reducing his demands to half a dozen fowls on account, and all the rest on the day of the marriage. Then, with the delightful feeling that he wouldn't do any work for a week, he went out to drop poison into the ears of Mr. Wiggett.

"Lost all her money!" said the startled Mr. Wiggett. "How?"

"I don't know how," said his friend. "Tidger told me, but made me promise not to tell a soul. But I couldn't help telling you, Wiggett, 'cause I know what you're after."

"Do me a favour," said the little man.

"I will," said the other.

"Keep it from Miller as long as possible. If you hear any one else talking of it, tell 'em to keep it from him. If he marries her I'll give you a couple of pints."

Mr. Smith promised faithfully, and both the Tidgers and Mrs. Pullen were surprised to find that Mr. Miller was the only visitor that evening. He spoke but little, and that little in a slow, ponderous voice intended for Mrs. Pullen's ear alone. He spoke disparagingly of money, and shook his head slowly at the temptations it brought in its train. Give him a crust, he said, and somebody to halve it with—a home-made crust baked by a wife. It was a pretty picture, but somewhat spoiled by Mrs. Tidger suggesting that, though he had spoken of halving the crust, he had said nothing about the beer.

"Half of my beer wouldn't be much," said the dealer, slowly.

"Not the half you would give your wife wouldn't," retorted Mrs. Tidger.

The dealer sighed and looked mournfully at Mrs. Pullen. The lady sighed in return, and finding that her admirer's stock of conversation seemed to be exhausted, coyly suggested a game of draughts. The dealer assented with eagerness, and declining the offer of a glass of beer by explaining that he had had one the day before yesterday, sat down and lost seven games right off. He gave up at the seventh game, and pushing back his chair, said that he thought Mrs. Pullen was the most wonderful draught-player he had ever seen, and took no notice when Mrs. Tidger, in a dry voice charged with subtle meaning, said that she thought he was.

"Draughts come natural to some people," said Mrs. Pullen, modestly. "It's as easy as kissing your fingers."

Mr. Miller looked doubtful; then he put his great fingers to his lips by way of experiment, and let them fall unmistakably in the widow's direction. Mrs. Pullen looked down and nearly blushed. The carpenter and his wife eyed each other in indignant consternation.

"That's easy enough," said the dealer, and repeated the offense.

Mrs. Pullen got up in some confusion, and began to put the draught-board away. One of the pieces fell on the floor, and as they both stooped to recover it their heads bumped. It was nothing to the dealer's, but Mrs. Pullen rubbed hers and sat down with her eyes watering. Mr. Miller took out his handkerchief, and going to the scullery, dipped it into water and held it to her head.

"Is it better?" he inquired.

"A little better," said the victim, with a shiver.

Mr. Miller, in his emotion, was squeezing the handkerchief hard, and a cold stream was running down her neck.

"Thank you. It's all right now."

The dealer replaced the handkerchief, and sat for some time regarding her earnestly. Then the carpenter and his wife displaying manifest signs of impatience, he took his departure, after first inviting himself for another game of draughts the following night.

He walked home with the air of a conqueror, and thought exultingly that the two thousand pounds were his. It was a deal after his own heart, and not the least satisfactory part about it was the way he had got the better of Wiggett.

He completed his scheme the following day after a short interview with the useful Smith. By the afternoon Wiggett found that his exclusive information was common property, and all Thatcham was marvelling at the fortitude with which Mrs. Pullen was bearing the loss of her fortune. With a view of being out of the way when the denial was published, Mr. Miller, after loudly expressing in public his sympathy for Mrs. Pullen and his admiration of her qualities, drove over with some pigs to a neighbouring village, returning to Thatcham in the early evening. Then hurriedly putting his horse up he made his way to the carpenter's.

The Tidgers were at home when he entered, and Mrs. Pullen flushed faintly as he shook hands.

"I was coming in before," he said, impressively, "after what I heard this afternoon, but I had to drive over to Thorpe."

"You 'eard it?" inquired the carpenter, in an incredulous voice.

"Certainly," said the dealer, "and very sorry I was. Sorry for one thing, but glad for another."

The carpenter opened his mouth and seemed about to speak. Then he checked himself suddenly and gazed with interest at the ingenuous dealer.

"I'm glad," said Mr. Miller, slowly, as he nodded at a friend of Mrs. Tidger's who had just come in with a long face, "because now that Mrs. Pullen is poor, I can say to her what I couldn't say while she was rich."

Again the astonished carpenter was about to speak, but the dealer hastily checked him with his hand.

"One at a time," he said. "Mrs. Pullen, I was very sorry to hear this afternoon, for your sake, that you had lost all your money. What I wanted to say to you now, now that you are poor, was to ask you to be Mrs. Miller. What d'ye say?"

Mrs. Pullen, touched at so much goodness, wept softly and said, "Yes." The triumphant Miller took out his handkerchief—the same that he had used the previous night, for he was not an extravagant man—and tenderly wiped her eyes.

"Well, I'm blowed!" said the staring carpenter.

"I've got a nice little 'ouse," continued the wily Mr. Miller. "It's a poor place, but nice, and we'll play draughts every evening. When shall it be?"

"When you like," said Mrs. Pullen, in a faint voice.

"I'll put the banns up to-morrow," said the dealer.

Mrs. Tidger's lady friend giggled at so much haste, but Mrs. Tidger, who felt that she had misjudged him, was touched.

"It does you credit, Mr. Miller," she said, warmly.

"No, no," said the dealer; and then Mr. Tidger got up, and crossing the room, solemnly shook hands with him.

"Money or no money, she'll make a good wife," he said.

"I'm glad you're pleased," said the dealer, wondering at this cordiality.

"I don't deny I thought you was after her money," continued the carpenter, solemnly. "My missus thought so, too."

Mr. Miller shook his head, and said he thought they would have known him better.

"Of course it is a great loss," said the carpenter. "Money is money."

"That's all it is, though," said the slightly mystified Mr. Miller.

"What I can't understand is," continued the carpenter, "'ow the news got about. Why, the neighbours knew of it a couple of hours before we did."

The dealer hid a grin. Then he looked a bit bewildered again.

"I assure you," said the carpenter, "it was known in the town at least a couple of hours before we got the letter."

Mr. Miller waited a minute to get perfect control over his features. "Letter?" he repeated, faintly.

"The letter from the lawyers," said the carpenter.

Mr. Miller was silent again. His features were getting tiresome. He eyed the door furtively.

"What-was-in-the letter?" he asked.

"Short and sweet," said the carpenter, with bitterness. "Said it was all a mistake, because they'd been and found another will. People shouldn't make such mistakes."

"We're all liable to make mistakes," said Miller, thinking he saw an opening.

"Yes, we made a mistake when we thought you was after Ann's money," assented the carpenter.

"I'm sure I thought you'd be the last man in the world to be pleased to hear that she'd lost it. One thing is, you've got enough for both."

Mr. Miller made no reply, but in a dazed way strove to realize the full measure of the misfortune which had befallen him. The neighbour, with the anxiety of her sex to be the first with a bit of news, had already taken her departure. He thought of Wiggett walking the earth a free man, and of Smith with a three-months' bill for twenty pounds. His pride as a dealer was shattered beyond repair, and emerging from a species of mist, he became conscious that the carpenter was addressing him.

"We'll leave you two young things alone for a bit," said Mr. Tidger, heartily. "We're going out. When you're tired o' courting you can play draughts, and Ann will show you one or two of 'er moves. So long."

A HARBOUR OF REFUGE

A waterman's boat was lying in the river just below Greenwich, the waterman resting on his oars, while his fare, a small, perturbed-looking man in seaman's attire, gazed expectantly up the river.

"There she is!" he cried suddenly, as a small schooner came into view from behind a big steamer. "Take me alongside."

"Nice little thing she is too," said the waterman, watching the other out of the corner of his eye as he bent to his oars. "Rides the water like a duck. Her cap'n knows a thing or two, I'll bet."

"He knows watermen's fares," replied the passenger coldly.

"Look out there!" cried a voice from the schooner, and the mate threw a line which the passenger skilfully caught.

The waterman ceased rowing, and, as his boat came alongside the schooner, held out his hand to his passenger, who had already commenced to scramble up the side, and demanded his fare. It was handed down to him.

"It's all right, then," said the fare, as he stood on the deck and closed his eyes to the painful language in which the waterman was addressing him. "Nobody been inquiring for me?"

"Not a soul," said the mate. "What's all the row about?"

"Well, you see, it's this way," said the master of the Frolic, dropping his voice. "I've been taking a little too much notice of a little craft down Battersea way—nice little thing, an' she thought I was a single man, dy'e see?"

The mate sucked his teeth.

"She introduced me to her brother as a single man," continued the skipper. "He asked me when the banns was to be put up, an' I didn't like to tell him I was a married man with a family."

"Why not?" asked the mate.

"He's a prize-fighter," said the other, in awe-inspiring tones; "'the Battersea Bruiser.' Consequently when he clapped me on the back, and asked me when the banns was to be, I only smiled."

"What did he do?" inquired the mate, who was becoming interested.

"Put 'em up," groaned the skipper, "an' we all went to church to hear 'em. Talk o' people walking over your grave, George, it's nothing to what I felt—nothing. I felt a hypocrite, almost. Somehow he found out about me, and I've been hiding ever since I sent you that note. He told a pal he was going to give me a licking, and come down to Fairhaven with us and make mischief between me and the missis."

"That 'ud be worse than the licking," said the mate sagely.

"Ah! and she'd believe him afore she would me, too, an' we've been married seventeen years," said the skipper mournfully.

"Perhaps that's"—began the mate, and stopped suddenly.

"Perhaps what?" inquired the other, after waiting a reasonable time for him to finish.

"H'm, I forgot what I was going to say," said the mate. "Funny, it's gone now. Well, you're all right now. You'd intended this to be the last trip to London for some time."

"Yes, that's what made me a bit more loving than I should ha' been," mused the skipper. "However, all's well that ends well. How did you get on about the cook? Did you ship one?"

"Yes, I've got one, but he's only signed as far as Fairhaven," replied the mate. "Fine strong chap he is. He's too good for a cook. I never saw a better built man in my life. It'll do your eyes good to look at him. Here, cook!"

At the summons a huge, close-cropped head was thrust out of the galley, and a man of beautiful muscular development stepped out before the eyes of the paralyzed skipper, and began to remove his coat.

"Ain't he a fine chap?" said the mate admiringly. "Show him your biceps, cook."

With a leer at the captain the cook complied. He then doubled his fists, and, ducking his head scientifically, danced all round the stupefied master of the Frolic.

"Put your dooks up," he cried warningly. "I'm going to dot you!"

"What the deuce are you up to, cook?" demanded the mate, who had been watching his proceedings in speechless amazement.

"Cook!" said the person addressed, with majestic scorn. "I'm no cook; I'm Bill Simmons, the 'Battersea Bruiser,' an' I shipped on this ere little tub all for your dear captin's sake. I'm going to put sich a 'ed on 'im that when he wants to blow his nose he'll have to get a looking-glass to see where to go to. I'm going to give 'im a licking every day, and when we get to Fairhaven I'm going to foller 'im 'ome and tell his wife about 'im walking out with my sister."

"She walked me out," said the skipper, with dry lips.

"Put 'em up," vociferated the "Bruiser."

"Don't you touch me, my lad," said the skipper, dodging behind the wheel. "Go an' see about your work—go an' peel the taters."

"Wot!" roared the "Bruiser."

"You've shipped as cook aboard my craft," said the skipper impressively. "If you lay a finger on me it's mutiny, and you'll get twelve months."

"That's right," said the mate, as the pugilist (who had once had fourteen days for bruising, and still held it in wholesome remembrance) paused irresolute. "It's mutiny, and it'll also be my painful duty to get up the shotgun and blow the top of your ugly 'ed off."

"Would it be mutiny if I was to dot YOU one?" inquired the "Bruiser," in a voice husky with emotion, as he sidled up to the mate.

"It would," said the other hastily.

"Well, you're a nice lot," said the disgusted "Bruiser," "you and your mutinies. Will any one of you have a go at me?"

There was no response from the crew, who had gathered round, and were watching the proceedings with keen enjoyment.

"Or all of yer?" asked the "Bruiser," raising his eyebrows.

"I've got no quarrel with you, my lad," the boy remarked with dignity, as he caught the new cook's eye.

"Go and cook the dinner,'" said the skipper; "and look sharp about it. I don't want to have to find fault with a young beginner like you; but I don't have no shirkers aboard—understand that."

For one moment of terrible suspense the skipper's life hung in the balance, then the "Bruiser," restraining his natural instincts by a mighty effort, retreated, growling, to the galley.

The skipper's breath came more freely.

"He don't know your address, I s'pose," said the mate.

"No, but he'll soon find it out when we get ashore," replied the other dolefully. "When I think that I've got to take that brute to my home to make mischief I feel tempted to chuck him overboard almost."

"It is a temptation," agreed the mate loyally, closing his eyes to his chief's physical deficiencies. "I'll pass the word to the crew not to let him know your address, anyhow."

The morning passed quietly, the skipper striving to look unconcerned as the new cook grimly brought the dinner down to the cabin and set it before him. After toying with it a little while, the master of the Frolic dined off buttered biscuit.

It was a matter of much discomfort to the crew that the new cook took his duties very seriously, and prided himself on his cooking. He was, moreover, disposed to be inconveniently punctilious about the way in which his efforts were regarded. For the first day the crew ate in silence, but at dinner-time on the second the storm broke.

"What are yer looking at your vittles like that for?" inquired the "Bruiser" of Sam Dowse, as that able-bodied seaman sat with his plate in his lap, eyeing it with much disfavour. "That ain't the way to look at your food, after I've been perspiring away all the morning cooking it."

"Yes, you've cooked yourself instead of the meat," said Sam warmly. "It's a shame to spoil good food like that; it's quite raw."

"You eat it!" said the "Bruiser" fiercely; "that's wot you've go to do. Eat it!"

For sole answer the indignant Sam threw a piece at him, and the rest of the crew, snatching up their dinners, hurriedly clambered into their bunks and viewed the fray from a safe distance.

"Have you 'ad enough?" inquired the "Bruiser," addressing the head of Sam, which protruded from beneath his left arm.

"I 'ave," said Sam surlily.

"And you won't turn up your nose at good vittles any more?" inquired the "Bruiser" severely.

"I won't turn it up at anything," said Sam earnestly, as he tenderly felt the member in question.

"You're the only one as 'as complained," said the "Bruiser." "You're dainty, that's wot you are. Look at the others—look how they're eating theirs!"

At this hint the others came out of their bunks and fell to, and the "Bruiser" became affable.

"It's wonderful wot I can turn my 'and to," he remarked pleasantly. "Things come natural to me that other men have to learn. You 'd better put a bit of raw beef on that eye o' yours, Sam."

The thoughtless Sam clapped on a piece from his plate, and it was only by the active intercession of the rest of the crew that the sensitive cook was prevented from inflicting more punishment.

From this time forth the "Bruiser" ruled the roost, and, his temper soured by his trials, ruled it with a rod of iron. The crew, with the exception of Dowse, were small men getting into years, and quite unable to cope with him. His attitude with the skipper was dangerously deferential, and the latter was sorely perplexed to think of a way out of the mess in which he found himself.

"He means business, George," he said one day to the mate, as he saw the "Bruiser" watching him intently from the galley.

"He looks at you worse an' worse," was the mate's cheering reply. "The cooking's spoiling what little temper he's got left as fast as possible."

"It's the scandal I'm thinking of," groaned the skipper; "all becos' I like to be a bit pleasant to people."

"You mustn't look at the black side o' things," said the mate; "perhaps you won't want to need to worry about that after he's hit you. I'd sooner be kicked by a horse myself. He was telling them down for'ard the other night that he killed a chap once."

The skipper turned green. "He ought to have been hung for it," he said vehemently. "I wonder what juries think they're for in this country. If I'd been on the jury I'd ha' had my way, if they'd starved me for a month!"

"Look here!" said the mate suddenly; "I've got an idea. You go down below and I'll call him up and start rating him. When I'm in the thick of it you come and stick up for him."

"George," said the skipper, with glistening eyes, "you're a wonder. Lay it on thick, and if he hits you I'll make it up to you in some way."

He went below, and the mate, after waiting for some time, leaned over the wheel and shouted for the cook.

"What do you want?" growled the "Bruiser," as he thrust a visage all red and streaky with his work from the galley.

"Why the devil don't you wash them saucepans up?" demanded the mate, pointing to a row which stood on the deck. "Do you think we shipped you becos we wanted a broken-nosed, tenth-rate prize-fighter to look at?"

"Tenth-rate!" roared the "Bruiser," coming out on to the deck.

"Don't you roar at your officer," said the mate sternly. "Your manners is worse than your cooking. You'd better stay with us a few trips to improve 'em."

The "Bruiser" turned purple, and shivered with impotent wrath.

"We get a parcel o' pot-house loafers aboard here," continued the mate, airily addressing the atmosphere, "and, blank my eyes! if they don't think they're here to be waited on. You'll want me to wash your face for you next, and do all your other dirty work, you—"

"George!" said a sad, reproving voice.

The mate started dramatically as the skipper appeared at the companion, and stopped abruptly.

"For shame, George!" said the skipper. "I never expected to hear you talk to anybody like that, especially to my friend Mr. Simmons."

"Your WOT? demanded the friend hotly.

"My friend," repeated the other gently; "and as to tenth-rate prize-fighters, George, the 'Battersea Bruiser' might be champion of England, if he'd only take the trouble to train."

"Oh, you're always sticking up for him," said the artful mate.

"He deserves it," said the skipper warmly. "He's always run straight, 'as Bill Simmons, and when I hear 'im being talked at like that, it makes me go 'ot all over."

"Don't you take the trouble to go 'ot all over on my account," said the "Bruiser" politely.

"I can't help my feelings, Bill," said the skipper softly.

"And don't you call me Bill," roared the "Bruiser" with sudden ferocity. "D'ye think I mind what you and your little tinpot crew say. You wait till we get ashore, my friend, and the mate too. Both of you wait!"

He turned his back on them and walked off to the galley, from which, with a view of giving them an object-lesson of an entertaining kind, he presently emerged with a small sack of potatoes, which he slung from the boom and used as a punching ball, dealing blows which made the master of the Frolic sick with apprehension.

"It's no good," he said to the mate; "kindness is thrown away on that man."

"Well, if he hits one, he's got to hit the lot," said the mate. "We'll all stand by you."

"I can't always have the crew follering me about," said the skipper dejectedly. "No, he'll wait his opportunity, and, after he's broke my head, he'll go 'ome and break up my wife's 'art."

"She won't break 'er 'art," said the mate confidently. "She and you'll have a rough time of it; p'raps it would be better for you if she did break it a bit, but she's not that sort of woman. Well, those of us as live longest'll see the most."

For the remainder of that day the cook maintained a sort of unnatural calm. The Frolic rose and fell on the seas like a cork, and the "Bruiser" took short unpremeditated little runs about the deck, which aggravated him exceedingly. Between the runs he folded his arms on the side, and languidly cursed the sea and all that belonged to it; and finally, having lost all desire for food himself, went below and turned in.

He stayed in his bunk the whole of the next day and night, awaking early the following morning to the pleasant fact that the motion had ceased, and that the sides and floor of the fo'c'sle were in the places where people of regular habits would expect to find them. The other bunks were empty, and, after a toilet hastened by a yearning for nourishment, he ran up on deck.

Day had just broken, and he found to his surprise that the voyage was over, and the schooner in a small harbour, lying alongside a stone quay. A few unloaded trucks stood on a railway line which ran from the harbour to the town clustered behind it, but there was no sign of work or life; the good people of the place evidently being comfortably in their beds, and in no hurry to quit them.

The "Bruiser," with a happy smile on his face, surveyed the scene, sniffing with joy the smell of the land as it came fresh and sweet from the hills at the back of the town. There was only one thing wanting to complete his happiness—the skipper.

"Where's the cap'n?" he demanded of Dowse, who was methodically coiling a line.

"Just gone 'ome," replied Dowse shortly.

In a great hurry the "Bruiser" sprang on to the side and stepped ashore, glancing keenly in every direction for his prey. There was no sign of it, and he ran a little way up the road until he saw the approaching figure of a man, from whom he hoped to obtain information. Then, happening to look back, he saw the masts of the schooner gliding by the quay, and, retracing his steps a little, perceived, to his intense surprise, the figure of the skipper standing by the wheel.

"Ta, ta, cookie!" cried the skipper cheerily.

Angry and puzzled the "Bruiser" ran back to the edge of the quay, and stood owlishly regarding the schooner and the grinning faces of its crew as they hoisted the sails and slowly swung around with their bow pointing to the sea.

"Well, they ain't making a long stay, old man," said a voice at his elbow, as the man for whom he had been waiting came up. "Why, they only came in ten minutes ago. What did they come in for, do you know?"

"They belong here," said the "Bruiser"; "but me and the skipper's had words, and I'm waiting for 'im."

"That craft don't belong here," said the stranger, as he eyed the receding Frolic.

"Yes, it does," said the "Bruiser."

"I tell you it don't," said the other. "I ought to know."

"Look here, my friend," said the "Bruiser" grimly, "don't contradict me. That's the Frolic of Fairhaven."

"Very likely," said the man. "I don't know where she's from, but she's not from here."

"Why," said the "Bruiser," and his voice shook, "ain't this Fairhaven?"

"Lord love you, no!" said the stranger; "not by a couple o' hundred miles it ain't. Wot put that idea into your silly fat head?"

The frantic "Bruiser" raised his fist at the description, but at that moment the crew of the Frolic, which was just getting clear of the harbour, hung over the stern and gave three hearty cheers. The stranger was of a friendly and excitable disposition, and, his evil star being in the ascendant that morning, he took off his hat and cheered wildly back. Immediately afterwards he obtained unasked the post of whipping-boy to the master of the Frolic, and entered upon his new duties at once.

A LOVE KNOT

Mr. Nathaniel Clark and Mrs. Bowman had just finished their third game of draughts. It had been a difficult game for Mr. Clark, the lady's mind having been so occupied with other matters that he had had great difficulty in losing. Indeed, it was only by pushing an occasional piece of his own off the board that he had succeeded.

"A penny for your thoughts, Amelia," he said, at last.

Mrs. Bowman smiled faintly. "They were far away," she confessed.

Mr. Clark assumed an expression of great solemnity; allusions of this kind to the late Mr. Bowman were only too frequent. He was fortunate when they did not grow into reminiscences of a career too blameless for successful imitation.

"I suppose," said the widow, slowly—"I suppose I ought to tell you: I've had a letter."

Mr. Clark's face relaxed.

"It took me back to the old scenes," continued Mrs. Bowman, dreamily. "I have never kept anything back from you, Nathaniel. I told you all about the first man I ever thought anything of—Charlie Tucker?"

Mr. Clark cleared his throat. "You did," he said, a trifle hoarsely. "More than once."

"I've just had a letter from him," said Mrs. Bowman, simpering. "Fancy, after all these years! Poor fellow, he has only just heard of my husband's death, and, by the way he writes—"

She broke off and drummed nervously on the table.

"He hasn't heard about me, you mean," said Mr. Clark, after waiting to give her time to finish.

"How should he?" said the widow.

"If he heard one thing, he might have heard the other," retorted Mr. Clark. "Better write and tell him. Tell him that in six weeks' time you'll be Mrs. Clark. Then, perhaps, he won't write again."

Mrs. Bowman sighed. "I thought, after all these years, that he must be dead," she said, slowly, "or else married. But he says in his letter that he has kept single for my sake all these years."

"Well, he'll be able to go on doing it," said Mr. Clark; "it'll come easy to him after so much practice."

"He—he says in his letter that he is coming to see me," said the widow, in a low voice, "to—to—this evening."

"Coming to see you?" repeated Mr. Clark, sharply. "What for?"

"To talk over old times, he says," was the reply. "I expect he has altered a great deal; he was a fine-looking fellow—and so dashing. After I gave him up he didn't care what he did. The last I heard of him he had gone abroad."

Mr. Clark muttered something under his breath, and, in a mechanical fashion, began to build little castles with the draughts. He was just about to add to an already swaying structure when a thundering rat-tat-tat at the door dispersed the draughts to the four corners of the room. The servant opened the door, and the next moment ushered in Mrs. Bowman's visitor.

A tall, good-looking man in a frock-coat, with a huge spray of mignonette in his button-hole, met the critical gaze of Mr. Clark. He paused at the door and, striking an attitude, pronounced in tones of great amazement the Christian name of the lady of the house.

"Mr. Tucker!" said the widow, blushing.

"The same girl," said the visitor, looking round wildly, "the same as the day she left me. Not a bit changed; not a hair different."

He took her extended hand and, bending over it, kissed it respectfully.

"It's—it's very strange to see you again, Mr. Tucker," said Mrs. Bowman, withdrawing her hand in some confusion.

"Mr. Tucker!" said that gentleman, reproachfully; "it used to be Charlie."

Mrs. Bowman blushed again, and, with a side glance at the frowning Mr. Clark, called her visitor's attention to him and introduced them. The gentlemen shook hands stiffly.

"Any friend of yours is a friend of mine," said Mr. Tucker, with a patronizing air. "How are you, sir?"

Mr. Clark replied that he was well, and, after some hesitation, said that he hoped he was the same. Mr. Tucker took a chair and, leaning back, stroked his huge mustache and devoured the widow with his eyes. "Fancy seeing you again!" said the latter, in some embarrassment. "How did you find me out?"

"It's a long story," replied the visitor, "but I always had the idea that we should meet again. Your photograph has been with me all over the world. In the backwoods of Canada, in the bush of Australia, it has been my one comfort and guiding star. If ever I was tempted to do wrong, I used to take your photograph out and look at it."

"I s'pose you took it out pretty often?" said Mr. Clark, restlessly. "To look at, I mean," he added, hastily, as Mrs. Bowman gave him an indignant glance.

"Every day," said the visitor, solemnly. "Once when I injured myself out hunting, and was five days without food or drink, it was the only thing that kept me alive."

Mr. Clark's gibe as to the size of the photograph was lost in Mrs. Bowman's exclamations of pity.

"I once lived on two ounces of gruel and a cup of milk a day for ten days," he said, trying to catch the widow's eye. "After the ten days—"

"When the Indians found me I was delirious," continued Mr. Tucker, in a hushed voice, "and when I came to my senses I found that they were calling me 'Amelia.'"

Mr. Clark attempted to relieve the situation by a jocose inquiry as to whether he was wearing a mustache at the time, but Mrs. Bowman frowned him down. He began to whistle under his breath, and Mrs. Bowman promptly said, "H'sh!"

"But how did you discover me?" she inquired, turning again to the visitor.

"Wandering over the world," continued Mr. Tucker, "here to-day and there to-morrow, and unable to settle down anywhere, I returned to Northtown about two years ago. Three days since, in a tramcar, I heard your name mentioned. I pricked up my ears and listened; when I heard that you were free I could hardly contain myself. I got into conversation with the lady and obtained your address, and after travelling fourteen hours here I am."

"How very extraordinary!" said the widow. "I wonder who it could have been? Did she mention her name?"

Mr. Tucker shook his head. Inquiries as to the lady's appearance, age, and dress were alike fruitless. "There was a mist before my eyes," he explained. "I couldn't realize it. I couldn't believe in my good fortune."

"I can't think—" began Mrs. Bowman.

"What does it matter?" inquired Mr. Tucker, softly. "Here we are together again, with life all before us and the misunderstandings of long ago all forgotten."

Mr. Clark cleared his throat preparatory to speech, but a peremptory glance from Mrs. Bowman restrained him.

"I thought you were dead," she said, turning to the smiling Mr. Tucker. "I never dreamed of seeing you again."

"Nobody would," chimed in Mr. Clark. "When do you go back?"

"Back?" said the visitor. "Where?"

"Australia," replied Mr. Clark, with a glance of defiance at the widow. "You must ha' been missed a great deal all this time."

Mr. Tucker regarded him with a haughty stare. Then he bent towards Mrs. Bowman.

"Do you wish me to go back?" he asked, impressively,

"We don't wish either one way or the other," said Mr. Clark, before the widow could speak. "It don't matter to us."

"We?" said Mr. Tucker, knitting his brows and gazing anxiously at Mrs. Bowman. "We?"

"We are going to be married in six weeks' time," said Mr. Clark.

Mr. Tucker looked from one to the other in silent misery; then, shielding his eyes with his hand, he averted his head. Mrs. Bowman, with her hands folded in her lap, regarded him with anxious solicitude.

"I thought perhaps you ought to know," said Mr. Clark.

Mr. Tucker sat bolt upright and gazed at him fixedly. "I wish you joy," he said, in a hollow voice.

"Thankee," said Mr. Clark; "we expect to be pretty happy." He smiled at Mrs. Bowman, but she made no response. Her looks wandered from one to the other—from the good-looking, interesting companion of her youth to the short, prosaic little man who was exulting only too plainly in his discomfiture.

Mr. Tucker rose with a sigh. "Good-by," he said, extending his hand.

"You are not going—yet?" said the widow.

Mr. Tucker's low-breathed "I must" was just audible. The widow renewed her expostulations.

"Perhaps he has got a train to catch," said the thoughtful Mr. Clark.

"No, sir," said Mr. Tucker. "As a matter of fact, I had taken a room at the George Hotel for a week, but I suppose I had better get back home again."

"No; why should you?" said Mrs. Bowman, with a rebellious glance at Mr. Clark. "Stay, and come in and see me sometimes and talk over old times. And Mr. Clark will be glad to see you, I'm sure. Won't you Nath—Mr. Clark?"

"I shall be—delighted," said Mr. Clark, staring hard at the mantelpiece. "De-lighted."

Mr. Tucker thanked them both, and after groping for some time for the hand of Mr. Clark, who was still intent upon the mantelpiece, pressed it warmly and withdrew. Mrs. Bowman saw him to the door, and a low-voiced colloquy, in which Mr. Clark caught the word "afternoon," ensued. By the time the widow returned to the room he was busy building with the draughts again.

Mr. Tucker came the next day at three o'clock, and the day after at two. On the third morning he took Mrs. Bowman out for a walk, airily explaining to Mr. Clark, who met them on the way, that they had come out to call for him. The day after, when Mr. Clark met them returning from a walk, he was assured that his silence of the day before was understood to indicate a distaste for exercise.

"And, you see, I like a long walk," said Mrs. Bowman, "and you are not what I should call a good walker."

"You never used to complain," said Mr. Clark; "in fact, it was generally you that used to suggest turning back."

"She wants to be amused as well," remarked Mr. Tucker; "then she doesn't feel the fatigue."

Mr. Clark glared at him, and then, shortly declining Mrs. Bowman's invitation to accompany them home, on the ground that he required exercise, proceeded on his way. He carried himself so stiffly, and his manner was so fierce, that a well-meaning neighbor who had crossed the road to join him, and offer a little sympathy if occasion offered, talked of the weather for five minutes and inconsequently faded away at a corner.

Trimington as a whole watched the affair with amusement, although Mr. Clark's friends adopted an inflection of voice in speaking to him which reminded him strongly of funerals. Mr. Tucker's week was up, but the landlord of the George was responsible for the statement that he had postponed his departure indefinitely.

Matters being in this state, Mr. Clark went round to the widow's one evening with the air of a man who has made up his mind to decisive action. He entered the room with a bounce and, hardly deigning to notice the greeting of Mr. Tucker, planted himself in a chair and surveyed him grimly. "I thought I should find you here," he remarked.

"Well, I always am here, ain't I?" retorted Mr. Tucker, removing his cigar and regarding him with mild surprise.

"Mr. Tucker is my friend," interposed Mrs. Bowman. "I am the only friend he has got in Trimington. It's natural he should be here."

Mr. Clark quailed at her glance.

"People are beginning to talk," he muttered, feebly.

"Talk?" said the widow, with an air of mystification belied by her color. "What about?"

Mr. Clark quailed again. "About—about our wedding," he stammered.

Mr. Tucker and the widow exchanged glances. Then the former took his cigar from his mouth and, with a hopeless gesture threw it into the grate.

"Plenty of time to talk about that," said Mrs. Bowman, after a pause.

"Time is going," remarked Mr. Clark. "I was thinking, if it was agreeable to you, of putting up the banns to-morrow."

"There—there's no hurry," was the reply.

"'Marry in haste, repent at leisure,'" quoted Mr. Tucker, gravely.

"Don't you want me to put 'em up?" demanded Mr. Clark, turning to Mrs. Bowman.

"There's no hurry," said Mrs. Bowman again. "I—I want time to think."

Mr. Clark rose and stood over her, and after a vain attempt to meet his gaze she looked down at the carpet.

"I understand," he said, loftily. "I am not blind."

"It isn't my fault," murmured the widow, drawing patterns with her toe on the carpet. "One can't help their feelings."

Mr. Clark gave a short, hard laugh. "What about my feelings?" he said, severely. "What about the life you have spoiled? I couldn't have believed it of you."

"I'm sure I'm very sorry," murmured Mrs. Bowman, "and anything that I can do I will. I never expected to see Charles again. And it was so sudden; it took me unawares. I hope we shall still be friends."

"Friends!" exclaimed Mr. Clark, with extraordinary vigor. "With him?"

He folded his arms and regarded the pair with a bitter smile; Mrs. Bowman, quite unable to meet his eyes, still gazed intently at the floor.

"You have made me the laughing-stock of Trimington," pursued Mr. Clark. "You have wounded me in my tenderest feelings; you have destroyed my faith in women. I shall never be the same man again. I hope that you will never find out what a terrible mistake you've made."

Mrs. Bowman made a noise half-way between a sniff and a sob; Mr. Tucker's sniff was unmistakable.

"I will return your presents to-morrow," said Mr. Clark, rising. "Good-by, forever!"

He paused at the door, but Mrs. Bowman did not look up. A second later the front door closed and she heard him walk rapidly away.

For some time after his departure she preserved a silence which Mr. Tucker endeavored in vain to break. He took a chair by her side, and at the third attempt managed to gain possession of her hand.

"I deserved all he said," she cried, at last. "Poor fellow, I hope he will do nothing desperate."

"No, no," said Mr. Tucker, soothingly.

"His eyes were quite wild," continued the widow. "If anything happens to him I shall never forgive myself. I have spoilt his life."

Mr. Tucker pressed her hand and spoke of the well-known refining influence a hopeless passion for a good woman had on a man. He cited his own case as an example.

"Disappointment spoilt my life so far as worldly success goes," he said, softly, "but no doubt the discipline was good for me."

Mrs. Bowman smiled faintly, and began to be a little comforted. Conversation shifted from the future of Mr. Clark to the past of Mr. Tucker; the widow's curiosity as to the extent of the latter's worldly success remaining unanswered by reason of Mr. Tucker's sudden remembrance of a bear-fight.

Their future was discussed after supper, and the advisability of leaving Trimington considered at some length. The towns and villages of England were at their disposal; Mr. Tucker's business, it appeared, being independent of place. He drew a picture of life in a bungalow with modern improvements at some seaside town, and, the cloth having been removed, took out his pocket-book and, extracting an old envelope, drew plans on the back.

It was a delightful pastime and made Mrs. Bowman feel that she was twenty and beginning life again. She toyed with the pocket-book and complimented Mr. Tucker on his skill as a draughtsman.

A letter or two fell out and she replaced them. Then a small newspaper cutting, which had fluttered out with them, met her eye.

"A little veranda with roses climbing up it," murmured Mr. Tucker, still drawing, "and a couple of—"

His pencil was arrested by an odd, gasping noise from the window. He looked up and saw her sitting stiffly in her chair. Her face seemed to have swollen and to be colored in patches; her eyes were round and amazed.

"Aren't you well?" he inquired, rising in disorder.

Mrs. Bowman opened her lips, but no sound came from them. Then she gave a long, shivering sigh.

"Heat of the room too much for you?" inquired the other, anxiously.

Mrs. Bowman took another long, shivering breath. Still incapable of speech, she took the slip of paper in her trembling fingers and an involuntary exclamation of dismay broke from Mr. Tucker. She dabbed fiercely at her burning eyes with her handkerchief and read it again.

"TUCKER.—If this should meet the eye of Charles Tucker, who knew Amelia Wyborn twenty-five years ago, he will hear of something greatly to his advantage by communicating with N. C., Royal Hotel, Northtown."

Mrs. Bowman found speech at last. "N. C.—Nathaniel Clark," she said, in broken tones. "So that is where he went last month. Oh, what a fool I've been! Oh, what a simple fool!"

Mr. Tucker gave a deprecatory cough. "I—I had forgotten it was there," he said, nervously.

"Yes," breathed the widow, "I can quite believe that."

"I was going to show you later on," declared the other, regarding her carefully. "I was, really. I couldn't bear the idea of keeping a secret from you long."

Mrs. Bowman smiled—a terrible smile. "The audacity of the man," she broke out, "to stand there and lecture me on my behavior. To talk about his spoilt life, and all the time—"

She got up and walked about the room, angrily brushing aside the proffered attentions of Mr. Tucker.

"Laughing-stock of Trimington, is he?" she stormed. "He shall be more than that before I have done with him. The wickedness of the man; the artfulness!"

"That's what I thought," said Mr. Tucker, shaking his head. "I said to him—"

"You're as bad," said the widow, turning on him fiercely. "All the time you two men were talking at each other you were laughing in your sleeves at me. And I sat there like a child taking it all in. I've no doubt you met every night and arranged what you were to do next day."

Mr. Tucker's lips twitched. "I would do more than that to win you, Amelia," he said, humbly.

"You'll have to," was the grim reply. "Now I want to hear all about this from the beginning. And don't keep anything from me, or it'll be the worse for you."

She sat down again and motioned him to proceed.

"When I saw the advertisement in the Northtown Chronicle," began Mr. Tucker, in husky voice, "I danced with—"

"Never mind about that," interrupted the widow, dryly.

"I went to the hotel and saw Mr. Clark," resumed Mr. Tucker, somewhat crestfallen. "When I heard that you were a widow, all the old times came back to me again. The years fell from me like a mantle. Once again I saw myself walking with you over the footpath to Cooper's farm; once again I felt your hand in mine. Your voice sounded in my ears—"

"You saw Mr. Clark," the widow reminded him.

"He had heard all about our early love from you," said Mr. Tucker, "and as a last desperate chance for freedom he had come down to try and hunt me up, and induce me to take you off his hands."

Mrs. Bowman uttered a smothered exclamation.

"He tempted me for two days," said Mr. Tucker, gravely. "The temptation was too great and I fell. Besides that, I wanted to rescue you from the clutches of such a man."

"Why didn't he tell me himself?" inquired the widow.

"Just what I asked him," said the other, "but he said that you were much too fond of him to give him up. He is not worthy of you, Amelia; he is fickle. He has got his eye on another lady."

"WHAT?" said the widow, with sudden loudness.

Mr. Tucker nodded mournfully. "Miss Hackbutt," he said, slowly. "I saw her the other day, and what he can see in her I can't think."

"Miss Hackbutt?" repeated the widow in a smothered voice. "Miss—" She got up and began to pace the room again.

"He must be blind," said Mr. Tucker, positively.

Mrs. Bowman stopped suddenly and stood regarding him. There was a light in her eye which made him feel anything but comfortable. He was glad when she transferred her gaze to the clock. She looked at it so long that he murmured something about going.

"Good-by," she said.

Mr. Tucker began to repeat his excuses, but she interrupted him. "Not now," she said, decidedly. "I'm tired. Good-night."

Mr. Tucker pressed her hand. "Good-night," he said, tenderly. "I am afraid the excitement has been too much for you. May I come round at the usual time to-morrow?"

"Yes," said the widow.

She took the advertisement from the table and, folding it carefully, placed it in her purse. Mr. Tucker withdrew as she looked up.

He walked back to the "George" deep in thought, and over a couple of pipes in bed thought over the events of the evening. He fell asleep at last and dreamed that he and Miss Hackbutt were being united in the bonds of holy matrimony by the Rev. Nathaniel Clark.

The vague misgivings of the previous night disappeared in the morning sunshine. He shaved carefully and spent some time in the selection of a tie.

Over an excellent breakfast he arranged further explanations and excuses for the appeasement of Mrs. Bowman.

He was still engaged on the task when he started to call on her. Half-way to the house he arrived at the conclusion that he was looking too cheerful. His face took on an expression of deep seriousness, only to give way the next moment to one of the blankest amazement. In front of him, and approaching with faltering steps, was Mr. Clark, and leaning trustfully on his arm the comfortable figure of Mrs. Bowman. Her brow was unruffled and her lips smiling.

"Beautiful morning," she said, pleasantly, as they met.

"Lovely!" murmured the wondering Mr. Tucker, trying, but in vain, to catch the eye of Mr. Clark.

"I have been paying an early visit," said the widow, still smiling. "I surprised you, didn't I, Nathaniel?"

"You did," said Mr. Clark, in an unearthly voice.

"We got talking about last night," continued the widow, "and Nathaniel started pleading with me to give him another chance. I suppose that I am softhearted, but he was so miserable—You were never so miserable in your life before, were you, Nathaniel?"

"Never," said Mr. Clark, in the same strange voice.

"He was so wretched that at last I gave way," said Mrs. Bowman, with a simper. "Poor fellow, it was such a shock to him that he hasn't got back his cheerfulness yet."

Mr. Tucker said, "Indeed!"

"He'll be all right soon," said Mrs. Bowman, in confidential tones. "We are on the way to put our banns up, and once that is done he will feel safe. You are not really afraid of losing me again, are you, Nathaniel?"

Mr. Clark shook his head, and, meeting the eye of Mr. Tucker in the process, favored him with a glance of such utter venom that the latter was almost startled.

"Good-by, Mr. Tucker," said the widow, holding out her hand. "Nathaniel did think of inviting you to come to my wedding, but perhaps it is best not. However, if I alter my mind, I will get him to advertise for you again. Good-by."

She placed her arm in Mr. Clark's again, and led him slowly away. Mr. Tucker stood watching them for some time, and then, with a glance in the direction of the "George," where he had left a very small portmanteau, he did a hasty sum in comparative values and made his way to the railway-station.

A LOVE PASSAGE

The mate was leaning against the side of the schooner, idly watching a few red-coated linesmen lounging on the Tower Quay. Careful mariners were getting out their side-lights, and careless lightermen were progressing by easy bumps from craft to craft on their way up the river.

A tug, half burying itself in its own swell, rushed panting by, and a faint scream came from aboard an approaching skiff as it tossed in the wash.

"JESSICA ahoy!" bawled a voice from the skiff as she came rapidly alongside.

The mate, roused from his reverie, mechanically caught the line and made it fast, moving with alacrity as he saw that the captain's daughter was one of the occupants. Before he had got over his surprise she was on deck with her boxes, and the captain was paying off the watermen.

"You've seen my daughter Hetty afore, haven't you?" said the skipper.
"She's coming with us this trip. You'd better go down and make up her bed, Jack, in that spare bunk."

"Ay, ay," said the mate dutifully, moving off.

"Thank you, I'll do it myself," said the scandalised Hetty, stepping forward hastily.

"As you please," said the skipper, leading the way below. "Let's have a light on, Jack."

The mate struck a match on his boot, and lit the lamp.

"There's a few things in there'll want moving," said the skipper, as he opened the door. "I don't know where we're to keep the onions now, Jack."

"We'll find a place for 'em," said the mate confidently, as he drew out a sack and placed it on the table.

"I'm not going to sleep in there," said the visitor decidedly, as she peered in. "Ugh! there's a beetle. Ugh!"

"It's quite dead," said the mate reassuringly. "I've never seen a live beetle on this ship."

"I want to go home," said the girl. "You've no business to make me come when I don't want to."

"You should behave yourself then," said her father magisterially. "What about sheets, Jack; and pillers?"

The mate sat on the table, and, grasping his chin, pondered. Then as his gaze fell upon the pretty, indignant face of the passenger, he lost the thread of his ideas.

"She'll have to have some o' my things for the present," said the skipper.

"Why not," said the mate, looking up again—"why not let her have your state-room?"

"'Cos I want it myself," replied the other calmly.

The mate blushed for him, and, the girl leaving them to arrange matters as they pleased, the two men, by borrowing here and contriving there, made up the bunk. The girl was standing by the galley when they went on deck again, an object of curious and respectful admiration to the crew, who had come on board in the meantime. She stayed on deck until the air began to blow fresher in the wider reaches, and then, with a brief good-night to her father, retired below.

"She made up her mind to come with us rather suddenly, didn't she?" inquired the mate after she had gone.

"She didn't make up her mind at all," said the skipper; "we did it for her, me an' the missus. It's a plan on our part."

"Wants strengthening?" said the mate suggestively.

"Well, the fact is," said the skipper, "it's like this, Jack; there's a friend o' mine, a provision dealer in a large way o' business, wants to marry my girl, and me an' the missus want him to marry her, so, o' course, she wants to marry someone else. Me an' 'er mother we put our 'eads together and decided for her to come away. When she's at 'ome, instead o' being out with Towson, direckly her mother's back's turned she's out with that young sprig of a clerk."

"Nice-looking young feller, I s'pose?" said the mate somewhat anxiously.

"Not a bit of it," said the other firmly. "Looks as though he had never had a good meal in his life. Now my friend Towson, he's all right; he's a man of about my own figger."

"She'll marry the clerk," said the mate, with conviction.

"I'll bet you she don't," said the skipper. "I'm an artful man, Jack, an' I, generally speaking, get my own way. I couldn't live with my missus peaceable if it wasn't for management."

The mate smiled safely in the darkness, the skipper's management consisting chiefly of slavish obedience.

"I've got a cabinet fortygraph of him for the cabin mantel-piece, Jack," continued the wily father. "He gave it to me o' purpose. She'll see that when she won't see the clerk, an' by-and-bye she'll fall into our way of thinking. Anyway, she's going to stay here till she does."

"You know your way about, cap'n," said the mate, in pretended admiration.

The skipper laid his finger on his nose, and winked at the mainmast.

"There's few can show me the way, Jack," he answered softly; "very few. Now I want you to help me too; I want you to talk to her a great deal."

"Ay, ay," said the mate, winking at the mast in his turn.

"Admire the fortygraph on the mantel-piece," said the skipper.

"I will," said the other.

"Tell her about a lot o' young girls you know as married young middle-aged men, an' loved 'em more an" more every day of their lives," continued the skipper.

"Not another word," said the mate. "I know just what you want. She shan't marry the clerk if I can help it."

The other turned and gripped him warmly by the hand. "If ever you are a father your elf, Jack," he said with emotion, "I hope as how somebody'll stand by you as you're standing by me."

The mate was relieved the next day when he saw the portrait of Towson.He stroked his moustache, and felt that he gained in good looks every time he glanced at it.

Breakfast finished, the skipper, who had been on deck all night, retired to his bunk. The mate went on deck and took charge, watching with great interest the movements of the passenger as she peered into the galley and hotly assailed the cook's method of washing up.

"Don't you like the sea?" he inquired politely, as she came and sat on the cabin skylight.

Miss Alsen shook her head dismally. "I've got to it," she remarked.

"Your father was saying something to me about it," said the mate guardedly.

"Did he tell the cook and the cabin boy too?" inquired Miss Alsen, flushing somewhat. "What did he tell you?"

"Told me about a man named Towson," said the mate, becoming intent on the sails, "and—another fellow."

"I took a little notice of HIM just to spoil the other," said the girl, "not that I cared for him. I can't understand a girl caring for any man. Great, clumsy, ugly things."

"You don't like him then?" said the mate.

"Of course not," said the girl, tossing her head.

"And yet they 've sent you to sea to get out of his way," said the mate meditatively. "Well, the best thing you can do" His hardihood failed him at the pitch.

"Go on," said the girl.

 "Well, it's this way," said the mate, coughing; "they've sent you to sea to get you out of this fellow's way, so if you fall in love with somebody on the ship they'll send you home again."

"So they will," said the girl eagerly. "I'll pretend to fall in love with that nice-looking sailor you call Harry. What a lark!"

"I shouldn't do that," said the mate gravely.

"Why not?" said the girl.

"'Tisn't discipline," said the mate very firmly; "it wouldn't do at all.

He's before the mast."

"Oh, I see," remarked Miss Alsen, smiling scornfully.

"I only mean pretend, of course," said the mate, colouring. "Just to oblige you."

"Of course," said the girl calmly. "Well, how are we to be in love?"

The mate flushed darkly. "I don't know much about such things," he said at length; "but we'll have to look at each other, and all that sort of thing, you know."

"I don't mind that," said the girl.

"Then we'll get on by degrees," said the other. "I expect we shall both find it come easier after a time."

"Anything to get home again," said the girl, rising and walking slowly away.

The mate began his part of the love-making at once, and, fixing a gaze of concentrated love on the object of his regard, nearly ran down a smack. As he had prognosticated, it came easy to him, and other well-marked symptoms, such as loss of appetite and a partiality for bright colours, developed during the day. Between breakfast and tea he washed five times, and raised the ire of the skipper to a dangerous pitch by using the ship's butter to remove tar from his fingers.

By ten o'clock that night he was far advanced in a profound melancholy. All the looking had been on his side, and, as he stood at the wheel keeping the schooner to her course, he felt a fellow-feeling for the hapless Towson, His meditations were interrupted by a slight figure which emerged from the companion, and, after a moment's hesitation, came and took its old seat on the skylight.

"Calm and peaceful up here, isn't it?" said he, after waiting some time for her to speak. "Stars are very bright to-night."

"Don't talk to me," said Miss Alsen snappishly.

"Why doesn't this nasty little ship keep still? I believe it's you making her jump about like this."

"Me?" said the mate in amazement.

"Yes, with that wheel."

"I can assure you "—began the mate.

"Yes, I knew you'd say so," said the girl.

"Come and steer yourself," said the mate; "then you'll see."

Much to his surprise she came, and, leaning limply against the wheel, put her little hands on the spokes, while the mate explained the mysteries of the compass. As he warmed with his subject he ventured to put his hands on the same spokes, and, gradually becoming more venturesome, boldly supported her with his arm every time the schooner gave a lurch.

"Thank you," said Miss Alsen, coldly extricating herself, as the male fancied another lurch was coming. "Good-night."

She retired to the cabin as a dark figure, which was manfully knuckling the last remnant of sleep from its eyelids, stood before the mate, chuckling softly.

"Clear night," said the seaman, as he took the wheel in his great paws.

"Beastly," said the mate absently, and, stifling a sigh, went below and turned in.

He lay awake for a few minutes, and then, well satisfied with the day's proceedings, turned over and fell asleep. He was pleased to discover, when he awoke, that the slight roll of the night before had disappeared, and that there was hardly any motion on the schooner. The passenger herself was already at the breakfast-table.

"Cap'n's on deck, I s'pose?" said the mate, preparing to resume negotiations where they were broken off the night before. "I hope you feel better than you did last night."

"Yes, thank you," said she.

"You'll make a good sailor in time," said the mate.

"I hope not," said Miss Alsen, who thought it time to quell a gleam of peculiar tenderness plainly apparent in the mate's eyes. "I shouldn't like to be a sailor even if I were a man."

"Why not?" inquired the other.

"I don't know," said the girl meditatively; "but sailors are generally such scrubby little men, aren't they?"

"SCUBBY?" repeated the mate, in a dazed voice.

"I'd sooner be a soldier," she continued; "I like soldiers—they're so manly. I wish there was one here now."

"What for?" inquired the mate, in the manner of a sulky schoolboy.

"If there was a man like that here now," said Miss Alsen thoughtfully, "I'd dare him to mustard old Towson's nose."

"Do what?" inquired the astonished mate.

"Mustard old Towson's nose," said Miss Alsen, glancing lightly from the cruet-stand to the portrait.

The infatuated man hesitated a moment, and then, reaching over to the cruet, took out the spoon, and with a pale, determined face, indignantly daubed the classic features of the provision dealer. His indignation was not lessened by the behaviour of the temptress, who, instead of fawning upon him for his bravery, crammed her handkerchief to her mouth and giggled foolishly.

"Where's father," she said suddenly, as a step sounded above. "Oh, you will get it!"

She rose from her seat, and, standing aside to let her father pass, went on deck. The skipper sank on to a locker, and, raising the tea-pot, poured himself out a cup of tea, which he afterwards decanted into a saucer. He had just raised it to his lips, when he saw something over the rim of it which made him put it down again untasted, and stare blankly at the mantel-piece.

"Who the—what the—who the devil's done this?" he inquired in a strangulated voice, as he rose and regarded the portrait,

"I did," said the mate.

"You did?" roared the other. "You? What for?"

"I don't know," said the mate awkwardly. "Something seemed to come over me all of a sudden, and I felt as though I MUST do it."

"But what for? Where's the sense of it?" said the skipper.

The mate shook his head sheepishly.

"But what did you want to do such a monkey-trick FOR?" roared the skipper.

"I don't know," said the mate doggedly; "but it's done, ain't it? and it's no good talking about it."

The skipper looked at him in wrathful perplexity. "You'd better have advice when we get to port, Jack," he said at length; "the last few weeks I've noticed you've been a bit strange in your manner. You go an' show that 'ed of yours to a doctor."

The mate grunted, and went on deck for sympathy, but, finding Miss Alsen in a mood far removed from sentiment, and not at all grateful, drew off whistling. Matters were in this state when the skipper appeared, wiping his mouth.

"I've put another portrait on the mantel-piece, Jack," he said menacingly; "it's the only other one I've got, an' I wish you to understand that if that only smells mustard, there'll be such a row in this 'ere ship that you won't be able to 'ear yourself speak for the noise."

He moved off with dignity as his daughter, who had overheard the remark, came sidling up to the mate and smiled on him agreeably.

"He's put another portrait there," she said softly.

"You'll find the mustard-pot in the cruet," said the mate coldly.

Miss Alsen turned and watched her father as he went forward, and then, to the mate's surprise, went below without another word. A prey to curiosity, but too proud to make any overture, he compromised matters by going and standing near the companion.

"Mate!" said a stealthy whisper at the foot of the ladder.

The mate gazed calmly out to sea.

"Jack!" said the girl again, in a lower whisper than before.

The mate went hot all over, and at once descended. He found Miss Alsen, her eyes sparkling, with the mustard-pot in her left hand and the spoon in her right, executing a war-dance in front of the second portrait.

"Don't do it," said the mate, in alarm.

"Why not?" she inquired, going within an inch of it.

"He'll think it's me," said the mate.

"That's why I called you down here," said she; "you don't think I wanted you, do you?"

"You put that spoon down," said the mate, who was by no means desirous of another interview with the skipper.

"Shan't!" said Miss Alsen.

The mate sprang at her, but she dodged round the table. He leaned over, and, catching her by the left arm, drew her towards him; then, with her flushed, laughing face close to his, he forgot everything else, and kissed her.

"Oh!" said Hetty indignantly.

"Will you give it to me now?" said the mate, trembling at his boldness.

"Take it," said she. She leaned across the table, and, as the mate advanced, dabbed viciously at him with the spoon. Then she suddenly dropped both articles on the table and moved away, as the mate, startled by a footstep at the door, turned a flushed visage, ornamented with three streaks of mustard, on to the dumbfounded skipper.

"Sakes alive!" said that astonished mariner, as soon as he could speak; "if he ain't a-mustarding his own face now—I never 'card of such a thing in all my life. Don't go near 'im, Hetty. Jack!"

"Well," said the mate, wiping his smarting face with his handkerchief.

"You've never been took like this before?" queried the skipper anxiously.

"O'course not," said the mortified mate.

"Don't you say o'course not to me," said the other warmly, "after behaving like this. A straight weskit's what you want. I'll go an' see old Ben about it. He's got an uncle in a 'sylum. You come up too, my girl."

He went in search of Ben, oblivious of the fact that his daughter, instead of following him, came no farther than the door, where she stood and regarded her victim compassionately.

"I'm so sorry," she said "Does it smart?"

"A little," said the mate; "don't you trouble about me."

"You see what you get for behaving badly," said Miss Alsen judicially.

"It's worth it," said the mate, brightening.

"I'm afraid it'll blister," said she. She crossed over to him, and putting her head on one side, eyed the traces wisely. "Three marks," she said.

"I only had one," suggested the mate.

"One what?" enquired Hetty.

"Those," said the mate.

In full view of the horrified skipper, who was cautiously peeping at the supposed lunatic through the skylight, he kissed her again.

"You can go away, Ben," said the skipper huskily to the expert. "D'ye hear, you can go AWAY, and not a word about this, mind."

The expert went away grumbling, and the father, after another glance, which showed him his daughter nestling comfortably on the mate's right shoulder, stole away and brooded darkly over this crowning complication. An ordinary man would have run down and interrupted them; the master of the Jessica thought he could attain his ends more certainly by diplomacy, and so careful was his demeanour that the couple in the cabin had no idea that they had been observed—the mate listening calmly to a lecture on incipient idiocy which the skipper thought it advisable to bestow.

Until the mid-day meal on the day following he made no sign. If anything he was even more affable than usual, though his wrath rose at the glances which were being exchanged across the table.

"By the way, Jack," he said at length, "what's become of Kitty Loney?"

"Who?" inquired the mate. "Who's Kitty Loney?"

It was now the skipper's turn to stare, and he did it admirably.

"Kitty Loney," he said in surprise, "the little girl you are going to marry."

"Who are you getting at?" said the mate, going scarlet as he met the gaze opposite.

"I don't know what you mean," said the skipper with dignity. "I'm allooding to Kitty Loney, the little girl in the red hat and white feathers you introduced to me as your future."

The mate sank back in his seat, and regarded him with open-mouthed, horrified astonishment.

"You don't mean to say you've chucked 'er," pursued the heartless skipper, "after getting an advance from me to buy the ring with, too? Didn't you buy the ring with the money?"

"No," said the mate, "I—oh, no—of course—what on earth are you talking about?"

The skipper rose from his seat and regarded him sorrowfully but severely. "I'm sorry, Jack," he said stiffly, "if I've said anything to annoy you, or anyway hurt your feelings. O' course it's your business, not mine. P'raps you'll say you never heard o' Kitty Loney?"

"I do say so," said the bewildered mate; "I do say so."

The skipper eyed him sternly, and without another word left the cabin.

"If she's like her mother," he said to himself, chuckling as he went up the companion-ladder, "I think that'll do."

There was an awkward pause after his departure. "I'm sure I don't know what you must think of me," said the mate at length, "but I don't know what your father's talking about."

"I don't think anything," said Hetty calmly. "Pass the potatoes, please."

"I suppose it's a joke of his," said the mate, complying.

"And the salt," said she; "thank you."

"But you don't believe it?" said the mate pathetically.

"Oh, don't be silly," said the girl calmly. "What does it matter whether I do or not?"

"It matters a great deal," said the mate gloomily. "It's life or death to me."

"Oh, nonsense," said Hetty. "She won't know of your foolishness. I won't tell her."

"I tell you," said the mate desperately, "there never was a Kitty Loney.
What do you think of that?"

"I think you are very mean," said the girl scornfully; "don't talk to me any more, please."

"Just as you like," said the mate, beginning to lose his temper.

He pushed his plate from him and departed, while the girl, angry and resentful, put the potatoes back as being too floury for consumption in the circumstances.

For the remainder of the passage she treated him with a politeness and good humour through which he strove in vain to break. To her surprise her father made no objection, at the end of the voyage, when she coaxingly suggested going back by train; and the mate, as they sat at dummy-whist on the evening before her departure, tried in vain to discuss the journey in an unconcerned fashion.

"It'll be a long journey," said Hetty, who still liked him well enough to make him smart a bit, "What's trumps?"

"You'll be all right," said her father. "Spades."

He won for the third time that evening, and, feeling wonderfully well satisfied with the way in which he had played his cards generally, could not resist another gibe at the crestfallen mate.

"You'll have to give up playing cards and all that sort o' thing when you're married, Jack," said he.

"Ay, ay," said the mate recklessly, "Kitty don't like cards."

"I thought there was no Kitty," said the girl, looking up, scornfully.

"She don't like cards," repeated the mate. "Lord, what a spree we had. Cap'n, when we went to the Crystal Palace with her that night."

"Ay, that we did," said the skipper.

"Remember the roundabouts?" said the mate.

"I do," said the skipper merrily. "I'll never forget 'em."

"You and that friend of hers, Bessie Watson, lord how you did go on!" continued the mate, in a sort of ecstasy. The skipper stiffened suddenly in his chair. "What on earth are you talking about?" he inquired gruffly.

"Bessie Watson," said the mate, in tones of innocent surprise. "Little girl in a blue hat with white feathers, and a blue frock, that came with us."

"You're drunk," said the skipper, grinding his teeth, as he saw the trap into which he had walked.

"Don't you remember when you two got lost, an' me and Kitty were looking all over the place for you?" demanded the mate, still in the same tones of pleasant reminiscence.

He caught Hetty's eye, and noticed with a thrill that it beamed with soft and respectful admiration.

"You've been drinking," repeated the skipper, breathing hard. "How dare you talk like that afore my daughter?"

"It's only right I should know," said Hetty, drawing herself up. "I wonder what mother'll say to it all?"

"You say anything to your mother if you dare," said the now maddened skipper. "You know what she is. It's all the mate's nonsense."

"I'm very sorry, cap'n," said the mate, "if I've said anything to annoy you, or anyway hurt your feelings. O' course it's your business, not mine. Perhaps you'll say you never heard o' Bessie Watson?"

"Mother shall hear of her," said Hetty, while her helpless sire was struggling for breath.

"Perhaps you'll tell us who this Bessie Watson is, and where she lives?" he said at length.

"She lives with Kitty Loney," said the mate simply.

The skipper rose, and his demeanour was so alarming that Hetty shrank instinctively to the mate for protection. In full view of his captain, the mate placed his arm about her waist, and in this position they confronted each other for some time in silence. Then Hetty looked up and spoke.

"I'm going home by water," she said briefly.

Tattooing is a gift," said the night-watchman, firmly. "It 'as to be a gift, as you can well see. A man 'as to know wot 'e is going to tattoo an' 'ow to do it; there's no rubbing out or altering. It's a gift, an' it can't be learnt. I knew a man once as used to tattoo a cabin-boy all over every v'y'gc trying to learn. 'E was a slow, painstaking sort o' man, and the langwidge those boys used to use while 'e was at work would 'ardly be believed, but 'e 'ad to give up trying arter about fifteen years and take to crochet-work instead.

"Some men won't be tattooed at all, being proud o' their skins or sich-like, and for a good many years Ginger Dick, a man I've spoke to you of before, was one o' that sort. Like many red-'aired men 'e 'ad a very white skin, which 'e was very proud of, but at last, owing to a unfortnit idea o' making 'is fortin, 'e let hisself be done.

"It come about in this way: Him and old Sam Small and Peter Russet 'ad been paid off from their ship and was 'aving a very 'appy, pleasant time ashore. They was careful men in a way, and they 'ad taken a room down East India Road way, and paid up the rent for a month. It came cheaper than a lodging-'ouse, besides being a bit more private and respectable, a thing old Sam was always very pertickler about.

"They 'ad been ashore about three weeks when one day old Sam and Peter went off alone becos Ginger said 'e wasn't going with 'em. He said a lot more things, too; 'ow 'e was going to see wot it felt like to be in bed without 'aving a fat old man groaning 'is 'eart out and another one knocking on the mantelpiece all night with twopence and wanting to know why he wasn't being served.

"Ginger Dick fell into a quiet sleep arter they'd gone; then 'e woke up and 'ad a sip from the water-jug—he'd 'a had more, only somebody 'ad dropped the soap in it—and then dozed off agin. It was late in the afternoon when 'e woke, and then 'e see Sam and Peter Russet standing by the side o' the bed looking at 'im.

"'Where've you been?' ses Ginger, stretching hisself and yawning.

"'Bisness,' ses Sam, sitting down an' looking very important. 'While you've been laying on your back all day me an' Peter Russet 'as been doing a little 'ead-work.'

"'Oh!' ses Ginger. 'Wot with?'

"Sam coughed and Peter began to whistle, an' Ginger he laid still and smiled up at the ceiling, and began to feel good-tempered agin.

"'Well, wot's the business?' he ses, at last.

"Sam looked at Peter, but Peter shook 'is 'ead at him.

"It's just a little bit 'o bisness we 'appened to drop on,' ses Sam, at last, 'me an' Peter, and I think that, with luck and management, we're in a fair way to make our fortunes. Peter, 'ere, ain't given to looking on the cheerful side o' things, but 'e thinks so, too.'

"'I do,' ses Peter, 'but it won't be managed right if you go blabbing it to everybody.'

"'We must 'ave another man in it, Peter,' ses Sam; 'and, wot's more, 'e must 'ave ginger-coloured 'air. That being so, it's only right and proper that our dear old pal Ginger should 'ave the fust offer.'

"It wasn't often that Sam was so affeckshunate, and Ginger couldn't make it out at all. Ever since 'e'd known 'im the old man 'ad been full o' plans o' making money without earning it. Stupid plans they was, too, but the stupider they was the more old Sam liked 'em.

"'Well, wot is it?' asks Ginger, agin.

"Old Sam walked over to the door and shut it; then 'e sat down on the bed and spoke low so that Ginger could hardly 'ear 'im.

"'A little public-'ouse,' he ses, 'to say nothing of 'ouse properly, and a red-'aired old landlady wot's a widder. As nice a old lady as any one could wish for, for a mother.'

"For a mother!' ses Ginger, staring:

"'And a lovely barmaid with blue eyes and yellow 'air, wot 'ud be the red-'edded man's cousin,' ses Peter Russet.

"'Look 'ere,' ses Ginger, 'are you going to tell me in plain English wot it's all about, or are you not?'

"'We've been in a little pub down Bow way, me an' Peter,' ses Sam, 'and we'll tell you more about it if you promise to join us an' go shares. It's kep' by a widder woman whose on'y son—red-'aired son—went to sea twenty-three years ago, at the age o' fourteen, an' was never 'eard of arterwards. Seeing we was sailor-men, she told us all about it, an' 'ow she still 'opes for him to walk into 'er arms afore she dies.'

"'She dreamt a fortnit ago that 'e turned up safe and sound, with red whiskers,' ses Peter.

"Ginger Dick sat up and looked at 'em without a word; then 'e got up out o' bed, an' pushing old Sam out of the way began to dress, and at last 'e turned round and asked Sam whether he was drunk or only mad.

"'All right,' ses Sam; 'if you won't take it on we'll find somebody as will, that's all; there's no call to get huffy about it. You ain't the on'y red-'edded man in the world.'

"Ginger didn't answer 'im; he went on dressing, but every now and then 'e'd look at Sam and give a little larf wot made Sam's blood boil.

"'You've got nothin' to larf at, Ginger,' he ses, at last; 'the landlady's boy 'ud be about the same age as wot you are now; 'e 'ad a scar over the left eyebrow same as wot you've got, though I don't suppose he got it by fighting a chap three times 'is size. 'E 'ad bright blue eyes, a small, well-shaped nose, and a nice mouth.'

"'Same as you, Ginger,' ses Peter, looking out of the winder.

"Ginger coughed and looked thoughtful.

"'It sounds all right, mates,' 'e ses at last, 'but I don't see 'ow we're to go to work. I don't want to get locked up for deceiving.'

"'You can't get locked up,' ses Sam; 'if you let 'er discover you and claim you, 'ow can you get locked up for it? We shall go in an' see her agin, and larn all there is to larn, especially about the tattoo marks, and then—'

"'Tattoo marks!' ses Ginger.

"'That's the strong p'int,' ses Sam. ''Er boy 'ad a sailor dancing a 'ornpipe on 'is left wrist, an' a couple o' dolphins on his right. On 'is chest 'e 'ad a full-rigged ship, and on 'is back between 'is shoulder-blades was the letters of 'is name—C.R.S.: Charles Robert Smith.'

"'Well, you silly old fool,' ses Ginger, starting up in a temper, 'that spiles it all. I ain't got a mark on me.'

"Old Sam smiles at 'im and pats him on the shoulder. 'That's where you show your want of intelleck, Ginger,' he ses, kindly. 'Why don't you think afore you speak? Wot's easier than to 'ave 'em put on?'

"'Wot?' screams Ginger. 'Tattoo me! Spile my skin with a lot o' beastly blue marks! Not me, not if I know it. I'd like to see anybody try it, that's all.'

"He was that mad 'e wouldn't listen to reason, and, as old Sam said, 'e couldn't have made more fuss if they'd offered to skin 'im alive, an' Peter Russet tried to prove that a man's skin was made to be tattooed on, or else there wouldn't be tat-tooers; same as a man 'ad been given two legs so as 'e could wear trousers. But reason was chucked away on Ginger, an' 'e wouldn't listen to 'em.

"They started on 'im agin next day, but all Sam and Peter could say didn't move 'im, although Sam spoke so feeling about the joy of a pore wid-der woman getting 'er son back agin arter all these years that 'e nearly cried.

"They went down agin to the pub that evening, and Ginger, who said 'e was curious to see, wanted to go too. Sam, who still 'ad 'opes of 'im, wouldn't 'ear of it, but at last it was arranged that 'e wasn't to go inside, but should take a peep through the door. They got on a tram at Ald-gate, and Ginger didn't like it becos Sam and Peter talked it over between theirselves in whispers and pointed out likely red'-aired men in the road.

"And 'e didn't like it when they got to the Blue Lion, and Sam and Peter went in and left 'im outside, peeping through the door. The landlady shook 'ands with them quite friendly, and the barmaid, a fine-looking girl, seemed to take a lot o' notice of Peter. Ginger waited about outside for nearly a couple of hours, and at last they came out, talking and larfing, with Peter wearing a white rose wot the barmaid 'ad given 'im.

"Ginger Dick 'ad a good bit to say about keeping 'im waiting all that time, but Sam said that they'd been getting valuable information, an' the more 'e could see of it the easier the job appeared to be, an' then him an' Peter wished for to bid Ginger good-bye, while they went and 'unted up a red-'aired friend o' Peter's named Charlie Bates.

"They all went in somewhere and 'ad a few drinks first, though, and arter a time Ginger began to see things in a different light to wot 'e 'ad before, an' to be arf ashamed of 'is selfishness, and 'e called Sam's pot a loving-cup, an' kep' on drinking out of it to show there was no ill-feeling, although Sam kep' telling him there wasn't. Then Sam spoke up about tattooing agin, and Ginger said that every man in the country ought to be tattooed to prevent the smallpox. He got so excited about it that old Sam 'ad to promise 'im that he should be tattooed that very night, before he could pacify 'im.

"They all went off 'ome with their arms round each other's necks, but arter a time Ginger found that Sam's neck wasn't there, an' 'e stopped and spoke serious to Peter about it. Peter said 'e couldn't account for it, an' 'e had such a job to get Ginger 'ome that 'e thought they would never ha' got there. He got 'im to bed at last an' then 'e sat down and fell asleep waiting for Sam.

"Ginger was the last one to wake up in the morning, an' before 'e woke he kept making a moaning noise. His 'ead felt as though it was going to bust, 'is tongue felt like a brick, and 'is chest was so sore 'e could 'ardly breathe. Then at last 'e opened 'is eyes and looked up and saw Sam an' Peter and a little man with a black moustache.

"'Cheer up, Ginger,' ses Sam, in a kind voice, 'it's going on beautiful.'

"'My 'ead's splittin',' ses Ginger, with a groan, 'an' I've got pins an' needles all over my chest.'

"'Needles,' ses the man with the black moustache. 'I never use pins; they'd pison the flesh.'

"Ginger sat up in bed and stared at 'im; then 'e bent 'is 'ead down and squinted at 'is chest, and next moment 'e was out of bed and all three of 'em was holding 'im down on the floor to prevent 'im breaking the tattooer's neck which 'e'd set 'is 'eart upon doing, and explaining to 'im that the tattooer was at the top of 'is profession, and that it was only by a stroke of luck 'e had got 'im. And Sam reminded 'im of wot 'e 'ad said the night before, and said he'd live to thank 'im for it.

"''Ow much is there done?' ses Ginger, at last, in a desprit voice.

"Sam told 'im, and Ginger lay still and called the tattooer all the names he could think of; which took 'im some time.

"'It's no good going on like that, Ginger,' ses Sam. 'Your chest is quite spiled at present, but if you on'y let 'im finish it'll be a perfeck picter.'

"'I take pride in it,' ses the tattooer; 'working on your skin, mate, is like painting on a bit o' silk.'

"Ginger gave in at last, and told the man to go on with the job and finish it, and 'e even went so far as to do a little bit o' tattooing 'imself on Sam when he wasn't looking. 'E only made one mark, becos the needle broke off, and Sam made such a fuss that Ginger said any one would ha' thought 'e'd hurt 'im.

"It took three days to do Ginger altogether, and he was that sore 'e could 'ardly move or breathe and all the time 'e was laying on 'is bed of pain Sam and Peter Russet was round at the Blue Lion enjoying theirselves and picking up information. The second day was the worst, owing to the tattooer being the worse for licker. Drink affects different people in different ways, and Ginger said the way it affected that chap was to make 'im think 'e was sewing buttons on instead o' tattooing.

"'Owever 'e was done at last; his chest and 'is arms and 'is shoulders, and he nearly broke down when Sam borrowed a bit o 'looking-glass and let 'im see hisself. Then the tattooer rubbed in some stuff to make 'is skin soft agin, and some more stuff to make the marks look a bit old.

"Sam wanted to draw up an agreement, but Ginger Dick and Peter Russet wouldn't 'ear of it. They both said that that sort o' thing wouldn't look well in writing, not if anybody else happened to see it, that is; besides which Ginger said it was impossible for 'im to say 'ow much money he would 'ave the handling of. Once the tattooing was done 'e began to take a'most kindly to the plan, an' being an orfin, so far as 'e knew, he almost began to persuade hisself that the red-'aired landlady was 'is mother.

"They 'ad a little call over in their room to see 'ow Ginger was to do it, and to discover the weak p'ints. Sam worked up a squeaky voice, and pretended to be the landlady, and Peter pretended to be the good-looking barmaid.

"They went all through it over and over agin, the only unpleasantness being caused by Peter Russet letting off a screech every time Ginger alluded to 'is chest wot set 'is teeth on edge, and old Sam as the landlady offering Ginger pots o' beer which made 'is mouth water.

"'We shall go round to-morrow for the last time,' ses Sam, 'as we told 'er we're sailing the day arter. Of course me an' Peter, 'aving made your fortin, drop out altogether, but I dessay we shall look in agin in about six months' time, and then perhaps the landlady will interduce us to you.'

"'Meantime,' ses Peter Russet, 'you mustn't forget that you've got to send us Post Office money-orders every week.'

"Ginger said 'e wouldn't forget, and they shook 'ands all round and 'ad a drink together, and the next arternoon Sam and Peter went to the Blue Lion for a last visit.

"It was quite early when they came back. Ginger was surprised to see 'em, and he said so, but 'e was more surprised when 'e heard their reasons.

"It come over us all at once as we'd bin doing wrong,' Sam ses, setting down with a sigh.

"'Come over us like a chill, it did,' ses Peter.

"'Doing wrong?' ses Ginger Dick, staring. 'Wot are you talking about?'

"'Something the landlady said showed us as we was doin' wrong,' ses old Sam, very solemn; 'it come over us in a flash.'

"'Like lightning,' ses Peter.

"'All of a sudden we see wot a cruel, 'ard thing it was to go and try and deceive a poor widder woman,' ses Sam, in a 'usky voice; 'we both see it at once.'

"Ginger Dick looks at 'em 'ard, 'e did, and then, 'e ses, jeering like:

"'I 'spose you don't want any Post Office money-orders sent you, then?' he ses.

"'No,' says Sam and Peter, both together.

"'You may have 'em all,' ses Sam; 'but if you'll be ruled by us, Ginger, you'll give it up, same as wot we 'ave—you'll sleep the sweeter for it.'

"'Give it up!' shouts Ginger, dancing up an' down the room, 'arter being tattooed all over? Why, you must be crazy, Sam—wot's the matter with you?'

"'It ain't fair play agin a woman,' says old Sam, 'three strong men agin one poor old woman; that's wot we feel, Ginger.'

"'Well, I don't feel like it,' ses Ginger; 'you please yourself, and I'll please myself.'

"'E went off in a huff, an' next morning 'e was so disagreeable that Sam an' Peter went and signed on board a steamer called the Penguin, which was to sail the day arter. They parted bad friends all round, and Ginger Dick gave Peter a nasty black eye, and Sam said that when Ginger came to see things in a proper way agin he'd be sorry for wot 'e'd said. And 'e said that 'im and Peter never wanted to look on 'is face agin.

"Ginger Dick was a bit lonesome arter they'd gone, but 'e thought it better to let a few days go by afore 'e went and adopted the red-'aired landlady. He waited a week, and at last, unable to wait any longer, 'e went out and 'ad a shave and smartened hisself up, and went off to the Blue Lion.

"It was about three o'clock when 'e got there, and the little public-'ouse was empty except for two old men in the jug-and-bottle entrance. Ginger stopped outside a minute or two to try and stop 'is trembling, and then 'e walks into the private bar and raps on the counter.

"'Glass o' bitter, ma'am, please,' he ses to the old lady as she came out o' the little parlour at the back o' the bar.

"The old lady drew the beer, and then stood with one 'and holding the beer-pull and the other on the counter, looking at Ginger Dick in 'is new blue jersey and cloth cap.

"'Lovely weather, ma'am,' ses Ginger, putting his left arm on the counter and showing the sailor-boy dancing the hornpipe.

"'Very nice,' ses the landlady, catching sight of 'is wrist an' staring at it. 'I suppose you sailors like fine weather?'

"'Yes, ma'am,' ses Ginger, putting his elbows on the counter so that the tattoo marks on both wrists was showing. 'Fine weather an' a fair wind suits us.'

"'It's a 'ard life, the sea,' ses the old lady.

"She kept wiping down the counter in front of 'im over an' over agin, an' 'e could see 'er staring at 'is wrists as though she could 'ardly believe her eyes. Then she went back into the parlour, and Ginger 'eard her whispering, and by and by she came out agin with the blue-eyed barmaid.

"'Have you been at sea long?' ses the old lady.

"'Over twenty-three years, ma'am,' ses Ginger, avoiding the barmaid's eye wot was fixed on 'is wrists, 'and I've been shipwrecked four times; the fust time when I was a little nipper o' fourteen.'

"'Pore thing,' ses the landlady, shaking 'er 'ead. 'I can feel for you; my boy went to sea at that age, and I've never seen 'im since.'

"'I'm sorry to 'ear it, ma'am,' ses Ginger, very respectful-like. 'I suppose I've lost my mother, so I can feel for you.'

"'Suppose you've lost your mother!' ses the barmaid; 'don't you know whether you have?'

"'No,' ses Ginger Dick, very sad. 'When I was wrecked the fust time I was in a open boat for three weeks, and, wot with the exposure and 'ardly any food, I got brain-fever and lost my memory.'

"'Pore thing,' ses the landlady agin.

"'I might as well be a orfin,' ses Ginger, looking down; 'sometimes I seem to see a kind, 'and-some face bending over me, and fancy it's my mother's, but I can't remember 'er name, or my name, or anythink about 'er.'

"'You remind me o' my boy very much,' ses the landlady, shaking 'er 'ead; 'you've got the same coloured 'air, and, wot's extraordinary, you've got the same tattoo marks on your wrists. Sailor-boy dancing on one and a couple of dolphins on the other. And 'e 'ad a little scar on 'is eyebrow, much the same as yours.'

"'Good 'evins,' ses Ginger Dick, starting back and looking as though 'e was trying to remember something.

"'I s'pose they're common among seafaring men?' ses the landlady, going off to attend to a customer.

"Ginger Dick would ha' liked to ha' seen 'er abit more excited, but 'e ordered another glass o' bitter from the barmaid, and tried to think 'ow he was to bring out about the ship on his chest and the letters on 'is back. The landlady served a couple o' men, and by and by she came back and began talking agin.

"'I like sailors,' she ses; 'one thing is, my boy was a sailor; and another thing is, they've got such feelin' 'earts. There was two of 'em in 'ere the other day, who'd been in 'ere once or twice, and one of 'em was that kind 'earted I thought he would ha' 'ad a fit at something I told him.'

"'Ho,' ses Ginger, pricking up his ears, 'wot for?'

"'I was just talking to 'im about my boy, same as I might be to you,' ses the old lady, 'and I was just telling 'im about the poor child losing 'is finger—'

"'Losing 'is wot?' ses Ginger, turning pale and staggering back.

"'Finger,' ses the landlady. 'E was only ten years old at the time, and I'd sent 'im out to—Wot's the matter? Ain't you well?'

"Ginger didn't answer 'er a word, he couldn't. 'E went on going backwards until 'e got to the door, and then 'e suddenly fell through it into the street, and tried to think.

"Then 'e remembered Sam and Peter, and when 'e thought of them safe and sound aboard the Penguin he nearly broke down altogether, as 'e thought how lonesome he was.

"All 'e wanted was 'is arms round both their necks same as they was the night afore they 'ad 'im tattooed."

A MIXED PROPOSAL

Major Brill, late of the Fenshire Volununteers, stood in front of the small piece of glass in the hatstand, and with a firm and experienced hand gave his new silk hat a slight tilt over the right eye. Then he took his cane and a new pair of gloves, and with a military but squeaky tread, passed out into the road. It was a glorious day in early autumn, and the soft English landscape was looking its best, but despite the fact that there was nothing more alarming in sight than a few cows on the hillside a mile away, the Major paused at his gate, and his face took on an appearance of the greatest courage and resolution before proceeding. The road was dusty and quiet, except for the children playing at cottage doors, and so hot that the Major, heedless of the fact that he could not replace the hat at exactly the same angle, stood in the shade of a tree while he removed it and mopped his heated brow.

He proceeded on his way more leisurely, overtaking, despite his lack of speed, another man who was walking still more slowly in the shade of the hedge.

"Fine day, Halibut," he said, briskly; "fine day."

"Beautiful," said the other, making no attempt to keep pace with him.

"Country wants rain, though," cried the Major over his shoulder.

Halibut assented, and walking slowly on, wondered vaguely what gaudy color it was that had attracted his eye. It dawned on him at length that it must be the Major's tie, and he suddenly quickened his pace, by no means reassured as the man of war also quickened his.

"Halloa, Brill!" he cried. "Half a moment."

The Major stopped and waited for his friend; Halibut eyed the tie uneasily—it was fearfully and wonderfully made—but said nothing.

"Well?" said the Major, somewhat sharply.

"Oh—I was going to ask you, Brill—Confound it! I've forgotten what I was going to say now. I daresay I shall soon think of it. You're not in a hurry?"

"Well, I am, rather," said Brill. "Fact is— Is my hat on straight, Halibut?"

The other assuring him that it was, the Major paused in his career, and gripping the brim with both hands, deliberately tilted it over the right eye again.

"You were saying—" said Halibut, regarding this manoeuvre with secret disapproval.

"Yes," murmured the Major, "I was saying. Well, I don't mind telling an old friend like you, Halibut, though it is a profound secret. Makes me rather particular about my dress just now. Women notice these things. I'm—sha'nt get much sympathy from a confirmed old bachelor like you—but I'm on my way to put a very momentous question."

"The devil you are!" said the other, blankly.

"Sir!" said the astonished Major.

"Not Mrs. Riddel?" said Halibut.

"Certainly, sir," said the Major, stiffly. "Why not?"

"Only that I am going on the same errand," said the confirmed bachelor, with desperate calmness.

The Major looked at him, and for the first time noticed an unusual neatness and dressiness in his friend's attire. His collar was higher than usual; his tie, of the whitest and finest silk, bore a pin he never remembered to have seen before; and for the first time since he had known him, the Major, with a strange sinking at the heart, saw that he wore spats.

"This is extraordinary," he said, briefly. "Well, good-day, Halibut. Can't stop."

"Good-day," said the other.

The Major quickened his pace and shot ahead, and keeping in the shade of the hedge, ground his teeth as the civilian on the other side of the road slowly, but surely, gained on him.

It became exciting. The Major was handicapped by his upright bearing and short military stride; the other, a simple child of the city, bent forward, swinging his arms and taking immense strides. At a by-lane they picked up three small boys, who, trotting in their rear, made it evident by their remarks that they considered themselves the privileged spectators of a foot-race. The Major could stand it no longer, and with a cut of his cane at the foremost boy, softly called a halt.

"Well," said Halibut, stopping.

The man's manner was suspicious, not to say offensive, and the other had much ado to speak him fair.

"This is ridiculous," he said, trying to smile. "We can't walk in and propose in a duet. One of us must go to-day and the other to-morrow."

"Certainly," said Halibut; "that'll be the best plan."

"So childish," said the Major, with a careless laugh, "two fellows walking in hot and tired and proposing to her."

"Absurd," replied Halibut, and both men eyed each other carefully.

"So, if I'm unsuccessful, old chap," said the Major, in a voice which he strove to render natural and easy, "I will come straight back to your place and let you know, so as not to keep you in suspense."

"You're very good," said Halibut, with some emotion; "but I think I'll take to-day, because I have every reason to believe that I have got one of my bilious attacks coming on to-morrow."

"Pooh! fancy, my dear fellow," said the Major, heartily; "I never saw you look better in my life."

"That's one of the chief signs," replied Halibut, shaking his head. "I'm afraid I must go to-day."

"I really cannot waive my right on account of your bilious attack," said the Major haughtily.

"Your right?" said Halibut, with spirit.

"My right!" repeated the other. "I should have been there before you if you had not stopped me in the first place."

"But I started first," said Halibut.

"Prove it," exclaimed the Major, warmly.

The other shrugged his shoulders.

"I shall certainly not give way," he said, calmly. "This is a matter in which my whole future is concerned. It seems very odd, not to say inconvenient, that you should have chosen the same day as myself, Brill, for such an errand—very odd."

"It's quite an accident," asseverated the Major; "as a matter of fact, Halibut, I nearly went yesterday. That alone gives me, I think, some claim to precedence."

"Just so," said Halibut, slowly; "it constitutes an excellent claim."

The Major regarded him with moistening eyes. This was generous and noble. His opinion of Halibut rose. "And now you have been so frank with me," said the latter, "it is only fair that you should know I started out with the same intention three days ago and found her out. So far as claims go, I think mine leads."

"Pure matter of opinion," said the disgusted Major; "it really seems as though we want an arbitrator. Well, we'll have to make our call together, I suppose, but I'll take care not to give you any opportunity, Halibut, so don't cherish any delusions on that point. Even you wouldn't have the hardihood to propose before a third party, I should think; but if you do, I give you fair warning that I shall begin, too."

"This is most unseemly," said Halibut. "We'd better both go home and leave it for another day."

"When do you propose going, then?" asked the Major.

"Really, I haven't made up my mind," replied the other.

The Major shrugged his shoulders.

"It won't do, Halibut," he said, grimly; "it won't do. I'm too old a soldier to be caught that way."

There was a long pause. The Major mopped his brow again. "I've got it," he said at last.

Halibut looked at him curiously.

"We must play for first proposal," said the Major, firmly. "We're pretty evenly matched."

"Chess?" gasped the other, a whole world of protest in his tones.

"Chess," repeated the Major.

"It is hardly respectful," demurred Halibut. "What do you think the lady would do if she heard of it?"

"Laugh," replied the Major, with conviction.

"I believe she would," said the other, brightening. "I believe she would."

"You agree, then?"

"With conditions."

"Conditions?" repeated the Major.

"One game," said Halibut, speaking very slowly and distinctly; "and if the winner is refused, the loser not to propose until he gives him permission."

"What the deuce for?" inquired the other, suspiciously.

"Suppose I win," replied Halibut, with suspicious glibness, "and was so upset that I had one of my bilious attacks come on, where should I be? Why, I might have to break off in the middle and go home. A fellow can't propose when everything in the room is going round and round."

"I don't think you ought to contemplate marriage, Halibut," remarked the Major, very seriously and gently.

"Thanks," said Halibut, dryly.

"Very well," said the Major, "I agree to the conditions. Better come to my place and we'll decide it now. If we look sharp, the winner may be able to know his fate to-day, after all."

Halibut assenting, they walked back together. The feverish joy of the gambler showed in the Major's eye as they drew their chairs up to the little antique chess table and began to place their pieces ready for the fray. Then a thought struck him, and he crossed over to the sideboard.

"If you're feeling a bit off colour, Halibut," he said, kindly, "you'd better have a little brandy to pull yourself together. I don't wish to take a mean advantage."

"You're very good," said the other, as he eyed the noble measure of liquid poured out by his generous adversary.

"And now to business," said the Major, as he drew himself a little soda from a siphon.

"Now to business," repeated Halibut, rising and placing his glass on the mantel-piece.

The Major struggled fiercely with his feelings, but, despite himself, a guilty blush lent colour to the other's unfounded suspicions.

"Remember the conditions," said Halibut, impressively.

"Here's my hand on it," said the other, reaching over.

Halibut took it, and, his thoughts being at the moment far away, gave it a tender, respectful squeeze. The Major stared and coughed. It was suggestive of practice.

If the history of the duel is ever written, it will be found not unworthy of being reckoned with the most famous combats of ancient times. Piece after piece was removed from the board, and the Major drank glass after glass of soda to cool his heated brain. At the second glass Halibut took an empty tumbler and helped himself. Suddenly there was a singing in the Major's ears, and a voice, a hateful, triumphant voice, said,

"Checkmate!"

Then did his gaze wander from knight to bishop and bishop to castle in a vain search for succour. There was his king defied by a bishop—a bishop which had been hobnobbing with pawns in one corner of the board, and which he could have sworn he had captured and removed full twenty minutes before. He mentioned this impression to Halibut.

"That was the other one," said his foe. "I thought you had forgotten this. I have been watching and hoping so for the last half-hour."

There was no disguising the coarse satisfaction of the man. He had watched and hoped. Not beaten him, so the Major told himself, in fair play, but by taking a mean and pitiful advantage of a pure oversight. A sheer oversight. He admitted it.

Halibut rose with a sigh of relief, and the Major, mechanically sweeping up the pieces, dropped them one by one into the box.

"Plenty of time," said the victor, glancing at the clock. "I shall go now, but I should like a wash first."

The Major rose, and in his capacity of host led the way upstairs to his room, and poured fresh water for his foe. Halibut washed himself delicately, carefully trimming his hair and beard, and anxiously consulting the Major as to the set of his coat in the back, after he had donned it again.

His toilet completed, he gave a satisfied glance in the glass, and then followed the man of war sedately down stairs. At the hall he paused, and busied himself with the clothes-brush and hat-pad, modestly informing his glaring friend that he could not afford to throw any chances away, and then took his departure.

The Major sat up late that night waiting for news, but none came, and by breakfast-time next morning his thirst for information became almost uncontrollable. He toyed with a chop and allowed his coffee to get cold. Then he clapped on his hat and set off to Halibut's to know the worst.

"Well?" he inquired, as he followed the other into his dining-room.

"I went," said Halibut, waving him to a chair.

"Am I to congratulate you?"

"Well, I don't know," was the reply; "perhaps not just yet."

"What do you mean by that?" said the Major, irascibly.

"Well, as a matter of fact," said Halibut, "she refused me, but so nicely and so gently that I scarcely minded it. In fact, at first I hardly realized that she had refused me."

The Major rose, and regarding his poor friend kindly, shook and patted him lightly on the shoulder.

"She's a splendid woman," said Halibut. "Ornament to her sex," remarked the Major.

"So considerate," murmured the bereaved one.

"Good women always are," said the Major, decisively. "I don't think I'd better worry her to-day, Halibut, do you?"

"No, I don't," said Halibut, stiffly.

"I'll try my luck to-morrow," said the Major.

"I beg your pardon," said Halibut.

"Eh?" said the Major, trying to look puzzled.

"You are forgetting the conditions of the game," replied Halibut. "You have to obtain my permission first."

"Why, my dear fellow," said the Major, with a boisterous laugh. "I wouldn't insult you by questioning your generosity in such a case. No, no, Halibut, old fellow, I know you too well."

He spoke with feeling, but there was an anxious note in his voice.

"We must abide by the conditions," said Halibut, slowly; "and I must inform you, Brill, that I intend to renew the attack myself."

"Then, sir," said the Major, fuming, "you compel me to say—putting all modesty aside—that I believe the reason Mrs. Riddel would have nothing to do with you was because she thought somebody else might make a similar offer."

"That's what I thought," said Halibut, simply; "but you see now that you have so unaccountably—so far as Mrs. Riddel is concerned—dropped out of the running, perhaps, if I am gently persistent, she'll take me."

The Major rose and glared at him.

"If you don't take care, old chap," said Halibut, tenderly, "you'll burst something."

"Gently persistent," repeated the Major, staring at him; "gently persistent."

"Remember Bruce and his spider," smiled the other.

"You are not going to propose to that poor woman nine times?" roared his incensed friend.

"I hope that it will not be necessary," was the reply; "but if it is, I can assure you, my dear Brill, that I'm not going to be outclassed by a mere spider."

"But think of her feelings!" gasped the Major.

"I have," was the reply; "and I'm sure she'll thank me for it afterward. You see, Brill, you and I are the only eligibles in the place, and now you are out of it, she's sure to take me sooner or later."

"And pray how long am I to wait?" demanded the Major, controlling himself with difficulty.

"I can't say," said Halibut; "but I don't think it's any good your waiting at all, because if I see any signs that Mrs. Riddel is waiting for you I may just give her a hint of the hopelessness of it."

"You're a perfect Mephistopheles, sir!" bawled the indignant Major. Halibut bowed.

"Strategy, my dear Brill," he said, smiling; "strategy. Now why waste your time? Why not make some other woman happy? Why not try her companion, Miss Philpotts? I'm sure any little assistance—"

The Major's attitude was so alarming that the sentence was never finished, and a second later the speaker found himself alone, watching his irate friend hurrying frantically down the path, knocking the blooms off the geraniums with his cane as he went. He saw no more of him for several weeks, the Major preferring to cherish his resentment in the privacy of his house. The Major also refrained from seeing the widow, having a wholesome dread as to what effect the contemplation of her charms might have upon his plighted word.

He met her at last by chance. Mrs. Riddel bowed coldly and would have passed on, but the Major had already stopped, and was making wild and unmerited statements about the weather.

"It is seasonable," she said, simply.

The Major agreed with her, and with a strong-effort regained his composure.

"I was just going to turn back," he said, untruthfully; "may I walk with you?"

"I am not going far," was the reply.

With soldierly courage the Major took this as permission; with feminine precision Mrs. Riddel walked about fifty yards and then stopped. "I told you I wasn't going far," she said sweetly, as she held out her hand. "Goodby."

"I wanted to ask you something," said the Major, turning with her. "I can't think what it was.

They walked on very slowly, the Major's heart beating rapidly as he told himself that the lady's coldness was due to his neglect of the past few weeks, and his wrath against Halibut rose to still greater heights as he saw the cruel position in which that schemer had placed him. Then he made a sudden resolution. There was no condition as to secrecy, and, first turning the conversation on to indoor amusements, he told the astonished Mrs. Riddel the full particulars of the fatal game. Mrs. Riddel said that she would never forgive them; it was the most preposterous thing she had ever heard of. And she demanded hotly whether she was to spend the rest of her life in refusing Mr. Halibut.

"Do you play high as a rule?" she inquired, scornfully.

"Sixpence a game," replied the Major, simply.

The corners of Mrs. Riddel's mouth relaxed, and her fine eyes began to water; then she turned her head away and laughed. "It was very foolish of us, I admit," said the Major, ruefully, "and very wrong. I shouldn't have told you, only I couldn't explain my apparent neglect without."

"Apparent neglect?" repeated the widow, somewhat haughtily.

"Well, put it down to a guilty conscience," said the Major; "it seems years to me since I have seen you."

"Remember the conditions, Major Brill," said Mrs. Riddel, with severity.

"I shall not transgress them," replied the Major, seriously.

Mrs. Riddel gave her head a toss, and regarded him from the corner of her eyes.

"I am very angry with you, indeed," she said, severely. The Major apologized again. "For losing," added the lady, looking straight before her.

Major Brill caught his breath and his knees trembled beneath him. He made a half-hearted attempt to seize her hand, and then remembering his position, sighed deeply and looked straight before him. They walked on in silence.

"I think," said his companion at last, "that, if you like, you can get back at cribbage what you lost at chess. That is, of course, if you really want to."

"He wouldn't play," said the Major, shaking his head.

"No, but I will," said Mrs. Riddel, with a smile. "I think I've got a plan."

She blushed charmingly, and then, in modest alarm at her boldness, dropped her voice almost to a whisper. The Major gazed at her in speechless admiration and threw back his head in ecstasy. "Come round to-morrow afternoon," said Mrs. Riddel, pausing at the end of the lane. "Mr. Halibut shall be there, too, and it shall be done under his very eyes."

Until that time came the Major sat at home carefully rehearsing his part, and it was with an air of complacent virtue that he met the somewhat astonished gaze of the persistent Halibut next day. It was a bright afternoon, but they sat indoors, and Mrs. Riddel, after an animated description of a game at cribbage with Miss Philpotts the night before, got the cards out and challenged Halibut to a game.

They played two, both of which the diplomatic Halibut lost; then Mrs. Riddel, dismissing him as incompetent, sat drumming on the table with her fingers, and at length challenged the Major. She lost the first game easily, and began the second badly. Finally, after hastily glancing at a new hand, she flung the cards petulantly on the table, face downward.

"Would you like my hand, Major Brill?" she demanded, with a blush.

"Better than anything in the world," cried the Major, eagerly.

Halibut started, and Miss Philpotts nearly had an accident with her crochet hook. The only person who kept cool was Mrs. Riddel, and it was quite clear to the beholders that she had realized neither the ambiguity of her question nor the meaning of her opponent's reply.

"Well, you may have it," she said, brightly.

Before Miss Philpotts could lay down her work, before Mr. Halibut could interpose, the Major took possession of Mrs. Riddel's small white hand and raised it gallantly to his lips. Mrs. Riddel, with a faint scream which was a perfect revelation to the companion, snatched her hand away. "I meant my hand of cards," she said, breathlessly.

"Really, Brill, really," said Halibut, stepping forward fussily.

"Oh!" said the Major, blankly; "cards!"

"That's what I meant, of course," said Mrs. Riddel, recovering herself with a laugh. "I had no idea still—if you prefer—" The Major took her hand again, and Miss Philpotts set Mr. Halibut an example—which he did not follow—by gazing meditatively out of the window. Finally she gathered up her work and quitted the room. Mrs. Riddel smiled over at Mr. Halibut and nodded toward the Major.

"Don't you think Major Brill is somewhat hasty in his conclusions?" she inquired, softly.

"I'll tell Major Brill what I think of him when I get him alone," said the injured gentleman, sourly.

W.W. Jacobs – A Short Biography

William Wymark Jacobs was born on September 8, 1863 in the Wapping district of London, England. An author, humorist and dramatist, Jacobs is best remembered for the enduring classic tale of horror - "The Monkey's Paw".

As a youth, Jacobs grew up near the Wapping docks in London, where his father was a wharf manager. The family's first home was home was a house on a River Thames wharf.

The docklands setting would show up frequently in his later literary output. Jacobs, the wharf rat, and his three siblings lost their mother when they were all still young children. Their father, William Gage Jacobs, remarried and fathered a further seven children with his erstwhile housekeeper Ellen Florey. Although he grew up surrounded by poverty, Jacobs himself received a formal education in London, first at a private prep school and later at the Birkbeck Literary and Scientific Institute (now part of the University of London and known as Birkbeck College).

Jacobs' adult working life began with a clerical position at the Post Office Savings Bank. The job was not a stimulating one but Jacobs put his imagination to good use and started to write short stories, sketches and articles, many of which appeared in the Post Office house publication "Blackfriars Magazine."

Although Jacobs did receive his fair share of rejection slips at the beginning of his career, many works written during this period of clerical employment appeared in the "Idler" and "Today" magazines, both of which were edited by noted humorist Jerome K. Jerome, who had taken a liking to Jacobs' stories.

From 1898, Jacobs also published stories in "The Strand", a popular, monthly fiction and general interest magazine. The arrangement stayed in place for most of his life and many of the works in Jacobs' subsequent collections – including the nautical serialization A Master of Craft (1899-1900) - appeared there first.

Jacobs' first volume of collected works was published in 1896. Many Cargoes, a selection of sea-faring yarns, established Jacobs as a popular writer and humorist with a penchant for authentic dialogue and trick endings (critics of the day referred to him as the "O. Henry of the Waterfront").

A year later he published a novelette, The Skipper's Wooing, and in 1898 and another collection of short stories titled Sea Urchins. These works painted vivid, if imaginatively stretched, pictures of dockland and seafaring London with colourful characters (such as "The Night Watchman", Ginger Dick) that now seem archetypal.

Many of Jacobs' periodical publications and first editions were illustrated with woodcuts and ink drawings, as was still the custom at the turn of the 20th century. The author worked regularly with artists such as E.W. Kemble, who had illustrated Mark Twain's Adventures of Huckleberry Finn and Harriet Beecher Stowe's Uncle Tom's Cabin, and his good friend Will Owen, who eventually became a household name on the strength of his iconic Bisto Kids, Bovril and Lux Soap advertising posters.

By 1899, Jacobs was able to quit the post office and finally begin a career making a living as a full-time writer.

He married the noted suffragist Agnes Eleanor Williams (who had been jailed for her protest activities) in 1900. They set up a household in Loughton, Essex as well as living part of the year in central London. The couple went on to have five children together though their marriage was considered an unhappy one.

The publication of two short novels: At Sunwich Port (a romantic tale of rival sea captains in the fictional seaside community of Sunwich standing in for the actual East England community of Sandwich, Kent) and Dialstone Lane (another small town romance involving intrigue and buried treasure), in 1902 and 1904 respectively, cemented Jacobs' reputation as one of the leading British authors of the new century.

On the foundations of a continuing ability to write for his audience he was readily published though he never strayed too far from what was becoming his familiar, dependable style. There followed a string of further successful publications, including Captain's All (1905), Night Watches (1914), The Castaways (1916), and Sea Whispers (1926). Jacobs published eighteen books in all during his lifetime; thirteen collections and five novels.

As a storyteller, Jacobs is perhaps better remembered for a handful of brief tales of the supernatural than for his popular nautical-themed works. The most famous of these, The Monkey's Paw, originally appeared as part of the 1902 short story collection The Lady of the Barge. It is an economically written story about a shriveled talisman, a monkey's paw that brings grief and horror in the wake of all too literal wish granting. The story has been adapted for other media repeatedly, starting with a one-act play performed at London's Haymarket Theatre in 1903. There have been multiple film adaptations of the story in the modern era; some of us are familiar with its appearance in an episode of the popular animated series, The Simpsons.

Another macabre gem, The Toll-House, was published as part of the collection Sailor's Knots in 1909. Jacob's once again employs a sparse style to tell the story of a group of men who spend the night in a famously haunted house on a dare (a noticeably similar narrative concept was put to use in the much earlier play The Ghost of Jerry Bundler, which had launched Jacobs' parallel career as a dramatist back in 1899 when it was produced at the St. James Theatre in London). Innovative at the time of writing, these sparingly written, atmospheric ghost stories are now familiar classics of the supernatural genre.

Though prolific in his younger years, Jacobs' productivity dropped dramatically after the start of World War I. Yet even in self-imposed semi-retirement Jacobs was still recognized as a leading humorist, ranked alongside such writers as P. G. Wodehouse and George Birmingham. He enjoyed continuing influence and elevated status among his fellow writers as evidenced by these comments attributed to his colleague Henry James:

"Mr. Jacobs, I envy you. You are popular! Your admirable work is appreciated by a wide circle of readers; it has achieved popularity. Mine never goes into a second edition."

James' literary fortunes would, of course, change, but his back-handedly complimentary admiration is compelling evidence of Jacobs' reputation as a writer and humourist both for his audience and his perhaps more admired literary colleagues.

Though Jacobs would create little in the way of new work after 1911, he was still writing. In these later years, seemingly burnt out creatively, Jacobs concentrated more on writing dramatizations and adaptations of his existing stories, including Beauty and the Barge (a film version starring Margaret Rutherford was also released in 1937) and In the Dark (a one act play that is often performed pr published with The Monkey's Paw adaptation).

Though admired by loyal readers throughout his lifetime, Jacobs has been almost completely forgotten since. Critics are at a loss to name a single reason why - Jacobs is universally considered to be a fine and imaginative literary craftsman. But, as critic John Wain suggested in a 1960 essay, perhaps Jacobs' humour may have been too gentle to persist into the cruel and sarcastic modern era, his dry pokes at proletariat hardship no longer suiting the times.

Nonetheless, Jacobs' legacy remains solid: he continued Dickens' (a writer with whom he is also often compared) tradition for sharing working class stories in authentic vernacular. And polished narratives such as The Monkey's Paw set a standard for the clever use of horror in fiction and popular culture that endures to this day. Indeed recently his works have begun to show an increased demand and appreciation in a world that is constantly looking over its shoulder.

William Wymark Jacobs died in a North London nursing home in Hornsey Lane, Islington on September 1st, 1943, just a week before his 80th birthday.

NOVELS AND SHORT STORY COLLECTIONS
MANY CARGOES (SHORT STORIES) (1896)
THE SKIPPER'S WOOING (1897)
SEA URCHINS (SHORT STORIES) (1898) aka MORE CARGOES
A MASTER OF CRAFT (1900)
LIGHT FREIGHTS (SHORT STORIES) (1901)
THE LADY OF THE BARGE (SHORT STORIES) (1902)
AT SUNWICH PORT (1902)
DIALSTONE LANE (1902)
SALTHAVEN (1908)
CAPTAINS ALL (SHORT STORIES) (1911)
NIGHT WATCHERS (SHORT STORIES) (1914)
DEEP WATERS (SHORT STORIES) (1919)

SHORT STORIES (INCLUDING THOSE USED IN THE COLLECTIONS ABOVE)
A BENEFIT PERFORMANCE
A BLACK AFFAIR
A CASE OF DESERTION
A CHANGE OF TREATMENT
A CIRCULAR TOUR
A DISCIPLINARIAN
A DISTANT RELATIVE
A GARDEN PLOT
A GOLDEN VENTURE
A HARBOUR OF REFUGE
A LOVE KNOT
A LOVE PASSAGE
A MARKED MAN
A MIXED PROPOSAL
A RASH EXPERIMENT
A SAFETY MATCH
A SPIRIT OF AVARICE
A TIGER'S SKIN
ADMIRAL PETERS
AFTER THE INQUEST
ALF'S DREAM
AN ADULTERATION ACT
AN ELABORATE ELOPEMENT
AN INTERVENTION
AN ODD FREAK
ANGELS' VISITS
BACK TO BACK
BEDRIDDEN
THE WINTER OFFENSIVE
THE BEQUEST
BILL'S LAPSE

BILL'S PAPER CHASE
BLUNDELL'S IMPROVEMENT
THE BOATSWAIN'S WATCH
THE BOATSWAIN'S MATE
BOB'S REDEMPTION
BREAKING A SPELL
BREVET RANK
BROTHER HUTCHINS
THE BULLY OF THE "CAVENDISH"
THE CABIN PASSENGER
CAPTAIN ROGERS
THE CAPTAIN'S EXPLOIT
CAPTAINS ALL
THE CASTAWAY
THE CHANGELING
"CHOICE SPIRITS"
THE CONSTABLE'S MOVE
CONTRABAND OF WAR
THE CONVERT
THE COOK OF THE "GANNET"
CUPBOARD LOVE
DESERTED
DIRTY WORK
THE DISBURSEMENT SHEET
DIXON'S RETURN
DOUBLE DEALING
THE DREAMER
DUAL CONTROL
EASY MONEY
ESTABLISHING RELATIONS
FAIRY GOLD
FALSE COLOURS
FAMILY CARES
FINE FEATHERS
FOR BETTER OR WORSE
THE FOUR PIGEONS
FRIENDS IN NEED
GOOD INTENTIONS
THE GREY PARROT
THE GUARDIAN ANGEL
THE HEAD OF THE FAMILY
HER UNCLE
HIS LORDSHIP
HIS OTHER SELF
HOMEWARD BOUND
HUSBANDRY
IN BORROWED PLUMES
IN LIMEHOUSE REACH
IN MID-ATLANTIC
IN THE FAMILY
IN THE LIBRARY

JERRY BUNDLER
KEEPING UP APPEARANCES
KEEPING WATCH
THE LADY OF THE BARGE
LAWYER QUINCE
THE LOST SHIP
LOW WATER
MADE TO MEASURE
THE MADNESS OF MR. LISTER
"MANNERS MAKYTH MAN"
MATED
"MATRIMONIAL OPENINGS"
MIXED RELATIONS
MONEY CHANGERS
THE MONEY-BOX
THE MONKEY'S PAW
MRS. BUNKER'S CHAPERON
THE NEST EGG
ODD MAN OUT
THE OLD MAN OF THE SEA
OUTSAILED
OVER THE SIDE
PAYING OFF
THE PERSECUTION OF BOB PRETTY
PETER'S PENCE
PICKLED HERRING
PRIVATE CLOTHES
PRIZE MONEY
THE RESURRECTION OF MR. WIGGETT
THE RIVAL BEAUTIES
RULE OF THREE
SAM'S BOY
SAM'S GHOST
SELF-HELP
SENTENCE DEFERRED
SHAREHOLDERS
SKILLED ASSISTANCE
THE SKIPPER OF THE "OSPREY"
SMOKED SKIPPER
STEPPING BACKWARDS
STRIKING HARD
THE SUBSTITUTE
THE TEMPTATION OF SAMUEL BURGE
THE TEST
THE THREE SISTERS
TO HAVE AND TO HOLD
"THE TOLL-HOUSE"
TWIN SPIRITS
TWO OF A TRADE
THE UNDERSTUDY
THE UNKNOWN

THE VIGIL
WATCH-DOGS
THE WEAKER VESSEL
THE WELL
THE WHITE CAT

STAGE
THE GHOST OF JERRY BUNDLER (1899) (In London)

FILM ADAPTATIONS
A MASTER OF CRAFT (1922)
THE MONKEY'S PAW (1933)
OUR RELATIONS, a Laurel & Hardy film, "suggested by" to Jacobs' "The Money Box." (1936)
FOOTSTEPS IN THE FOG, from the short story The Interruption. (1955)